The Case Files of Henri Davenforth

Case File 3

Honor Raconteur

wait, that's not what I named the book
I didn't name it that either.
You don't suppose...

Magic
Outside
the
Box

only one other possible suspect

Sherard!

What? Wasn't it my turn?

Raconteur House

Published by Raconteur HouseMurfreesboro, TN

THE CASE FILES OF HENRI DAVENFORTH: Magic Outside the Box Case Files 3

A Raconteur House book/ published by arrangement with the author

For information address: www.raconteurhouse.com

Report 01: A Visit From the Queen

never bodes a good thing.

My chocolate was missing.

I stared at the vacant spot with a mixture of resignation and bemusement. Mostly resignation. I had no need to question who the thief might be. I knew quite well my erstwhile partner had taken the liberty. No doubt she'd make some blithe comment to cover her theft if I confronted her about it. I felt more bemused on *when* she'd absconded with the box. I'd barely put it in place two hours ago and I'd been in my lab most of the morning. Really, I knew professional thieves who would envy her skills.

Giving up, I assuaged my taste buds with the promise of stopping by Kingston's Chocolatory during lunch. For now, I had work to do.

It had been two weeks since the charms case that had unleashed an epidemic on the city. Kingston had not truly recovered from it—not yet—and areas of the population were still getting back on their feet. The Kingsmen were only at half strength. I'd participated in more than a few favors for Seaton, assisting as necessary, which doubled my work load some days. I'd not found it in me to complain. There was simply too much work for any one person, and if my assistance lessened another's suffering? Then of course I should render all aid. Jamie had stepped in several times as well, assisting the Kingsmen. It meant we hadn't seen much of each other, even though we lived in the same building.

I had hope we'd pull through this rough patch and find our equilibrium soon enough. It would just take a little more patience, a little more work, and we'd set the world to rights again.

The lab work Sanderson had not seen fit to do in my absence was piled up around me, and I patiently sorted through the thick pile of requests. Some of the work needed to percolate, and I was able to get three different things started, then run herd on them until I had the results. I lost time as I worked, writing up reports in a neat hand. The lab around me remained utterly still aside from the scratch-scratch of my pen against paper.

So, when my door abruptly opened, I just about leapt from my stool, heart trying to beat its way past my sternum. "Stonking deities, woman, are you trying to give me heart failure?"

Jamie quirked a smile at me as she paused at the safe line at the floor. "Not my fault you're easily startled. We have a guest."

"A guest?" I stood automatically to greet whoever waited behind her. Then I nearly swallowed my tongue. On my partner's heels stood Queen Regina, looking smartly put-together in a day dress of deep purple, her dark hair pinned simply up on her head, and a determined set to her jaw. Having grown up with both sister and mother, I knew the look of a woman vexed and internally groaned. This boded ill. If the queen herself had come down to my lab, I couldn't imagine it was to impart good news.

"Your Majesty. Please, do be seated." I pulled out one of my stools from underneath the table and offered it to her, which was a mediocre seat, but the best I could offer. She took it, looking about her curiously. I imagined she'd not seen the inside of a magical examiner's workspace before. My walls were lined with shelves harboring all sorts of chemicals, magical ingredients, books, and different forms used in reporting evidence. Her gloved hands rested lightly on the scarred worktable.

Raising her chin, she said in her cool contralto, "Dr. Davenforth. I realize it must be quite shocking to see your sovereign sitting here."

Shocking was a gross understatement. I managed a smile for her somehow. "Not at all. Well, to be frank, I am rather alarmed. The expression on your face inclines me to think something dire has occurred."

"You're quite correct. I came directly to Jamie because I'm quite wroth at the moment and I need her expertise. She maintains she'll not work the case without you, and indeed, you two have proven to be a formidable pair. I'm inclined to think you'll get to the bottom of this."

I took 'inclined' to mean we had no option but to give results. Or heads would roll. I gestured for Jamie to take my other chair. "Indeed. Might we have the particulars?"

"Royal Mage Burtchell is dead," Queen Regina informed us flatly.

A sharp breath tore out of my throat. That was preposterous!

Jamie held up a hand, stalling us both. "Wait, I don't know who that is."

"Joseph Burtchell was the royal mage who formerly held Sherard's position," Queen Regina said, a tic in the corner of her mouth. I'd seen kinder eyes on professional killers. "He was retired, had been for several years. A few health complications sent him into a semi-early retirement in the country, near the sea. He was one of the best and brightest—a joy to us. I counted him as my friend and confidant all through my childhood and into my young adult years. We still saw him on a regular basis via different social events."

I still mentally reeled. Joseph Burtchell was a legend—a powerhouse of magical power and excellent example of intelligence well applied. He was the epitome of what a royal mage should be. The man was not without his flaws—I understood him to be a terrible gambler, even in his sixties—but magically speaking, he had few peers. I couldn't wrap my head around the loss. "Forgive me, Your Majesty, this might be an obvious question. But your presence here inclines me to believe him murdered?"

Her head dipped in a sharp nod. "Yes. He was at home this morning and found by his housekeeper. You know of Sheffield?"

I winced in immediate understanding. Mercy, no wonder she was so hot under the collar. To Jamie, who had little experience of the world outside Kingston, I hastily explained in an undertone, "Sheffield is a very small community along the sea. It's more a vacation spot for the rich, in truth, and doesn't have much in the way of crime. Excellent for safe holidays, but bollocks for actual investigation. The police on hand would be quite out of their element for anything outside petty theft."

Queen Regina appeared satisfied I understood the depth of the problem. "No one there can give me any hint of what happened. They have no suspects, no clues, nothing. I'd send my Kingsmen, but as you well know, half of them are still recovering. Even if I had someone to spare, murder is not truly their specialty. I'd much rather send the two of you."

I quite understood her point. Jamie and I were much better equipped for a murder investigation than anyone in Sheffield. "If the murder occurred this morning, I hope no one has disturbed the scene overmuch or removed the body?"

"Joseph was removed to the nearby hospital, or so it was reported to me. But I gave strict instructions to leave everything as it was."

There was that, at least. I exchanged a glance with Jamie, not sure how she wanted to approach this.

"Your Majesty." Jamie leaned against the table's

edge, her eyes level with the queen's. "We're of course willing to investigate and get you some answers. I want two things. No, three. I want Sherard, a coroner from this station, and Officer Penny McSparrin."

"Done. You can have anything and everything you deem necessary to investigate. I'll speak with your captain myself. I want you in Sheffield by this evening."

Jamie nodded, not bothered by this order. "We'll need to be. The longer we wait, the colder the case becomes. I can't promise you we'll find the murderer, but we'll do our best."

Snorting, our queen gave her a dark smile. "I've seen your best, Jamie Edwards. I'd not wager against you. Dr. Davenforth, I've heard what she needs. Have you any requests?"

Did I dare ask to get rid of Sanderson? No, that was likely too petty. "I won't know that until I'm on scene. Do you know if he had any magical protections up around the property?"

"I believe he did. But the police were able to enter, so you should be able to as well."

That wasn't why I inquired, but I doubted anyone other than a magician would be able to supply the answers I needed. I'd wait and ask Seaton when he joined us. "If you'd kindly relay the order for RM Seaton to join us? I'll confer with him about our time for departure."

"Of course." She was still outraged, but the tension that had brought her to us appeared lessened to a slight degree. She wasn't as clenched, her hands no longer forming fists on her lap. She seemed less likely to burst to her feet and order executions in a burst of rage, at any rate.

"You've got your pad with you? Charged?" Jamie inquired. "We'll give you updates through it."

The queen softened another degree and managed a smile. "Thank you, Jamie. Dr. Davenforth. I know it's upsetting to have a mad queen drop in on you like this. I apologize for my behavior."

"Think nothing of it," I assured her gently. "We're used to sudden cases dropping in our laps, are we not? And I know the death of your friend is very distressing."

Her eyes became bright with unshed tears for a moment, her voice hoarse. "Indeed it is. Thank you. I'll leave now and speak with your captain. Please leave as soon as possible."

"We'll be on the road within the hour," Jamie promised.

"Thank you."

We all stood, exchanging bows. With a brittle inhalation of breath, she stormed out of my lab as suddenly as she'd entered it.

Jamie let out a low whistle. "I have no idea what idiot thought it a good idea to kill a retired royal mage, but when we catch him, his head is going to roll. Regina will make sure of it."

"If she doesn't hang, draw, and quarter him first." My money was more on the latter. "When you requested a coroner from here, I assume you meant Weber?"

"Yes. I know you trust his eye, and judging from your description of Sheffield, they probably don't have a coroner on hand." She quirked a brow at me in question.

I nodded. "From my understanding of the place, likely not. It doesn't have enough murders to justify keeping one. Very well, if you'll go and fetch Officer McSparrin? I'll collect Weber."

"Sounds fair. How far is Sheffield from here?"

"A good four-hour drive."

Lips pursed, she suggested, "Then we should stay there while we're working on the case. We'll burn too much time driving back and forth otherwise. There's hotels or something over there, right? You said it was a holiday spot."

"Yes, hotels aplenty. I'll get an expense stipend issued for us." It was better that I do such paperwork. Jamie's grasp on the written word was still a project in progress. "We'll all need to pack, then I suppose meet back here?"

"In an hour, if we can manage it. I really don't want to let the trail get any colder than it already is."

I did understand her point. "Yes, quite. Go. I'll meet you out back in an hour."

Her stride was smooth and quiet as she left the room. I'd not been able to make the comparison before, prior to meeting Clint, but I realized now she moved like a Felix. All economy in her movements, with an inherent grace I couldn't begin to emulate.

Not sure why my mind focused on her in such a manner, I shook the odd thought off and moved out the door. I had a great deal to do and a short time to manage it in.

Normally coordinating several adults to meet at a specific time and place took a small miracle and more than a little patience. The random holidays I'd taken with my family through the years bore testament. I was pleasantly surprised when I entered the parking lot of the station to find everyone already assembled. As I watched, Seaton put a suitcase into the boot of the car.

Weber stood nearby, in front of his own vehicle of choice—a larger touring sedan with a tall, enclosed back. We'd just gotten the first shipment of them in, although I'd yet to sit inside one. The coroners preferred them, as it was easier to manhandle a corpse into the larger compartment. Or so Weber once told me over coffee.

"Davenforth," Weber greeted, lifting a hand. He was not in his usual overalls of white, but instead dressed in a light suit, suitable to the warmer weather we currently suffered through. It set off his dark chocolate skin, giving the illusion he was about to drive off for holiday instead of work. "I thought I would drive in separately. After I give you my report, there won't be much need for me to stay."

"Quite right," I agreed. There was no need to keep the man out in Sheffield when he had work of his own waiting for him here. "I imagine you can do the necessary work tomorrow and return in the evening."

"My thought exactly. If it's all the same, I'll follow you in."

I gave him a nod and towed my suitcase along with me. As I came in close, my heart fell a few rungs. Oh dear. Jamie had chosen a touring car, the longer sedan meant to hold four people (five at a push), with a larger boot in the back. It was meant for people to use on extended trips, and indeed this qualified, so it gave enough room for all four of us to travel. The part worrying me was that *Jamie* held the keys. I glared at Seaton in silent recrimination. Why hadn't he stopped her?

Oblivious to my unease, McSparrin greeted me smartly. "Doctor. We've room in the boot for your suitcase. Jamie and I loaded up your usual equipment already, but tell us if we missed anything."

"Thank you. Let me check." I glared at Seaton again as I passed him, and he grinned back at me in amusement. So he'd known what he'd done, but didn't regret it? He was in quite the mood, then. He knew as well as I what a madwoman she was behind the wheel.

I checked over the packed bags but could find no fault with the ladies' selection. I couldn't think of anything they'd missed. Satisfied, I loaded in my suitcase and tied it all down with the net. As I worked, a certain purple Felix hopped onto the back of the seat and watched me curiously. Startled, I paused and looked at him oddly. "Clint? Why are you here?"

"I can't leave him home alone for however long this takes," Jamie pointed out to me. "You remember what he was like after I was quarantined for so long? The separation anxiety was no joke. And he's promised to be good, haven't you, love?"

Clint preened at her, attempting to look angelic. I say attempt because he utterly failed.

Eyeing him, I debated putting my foot down. But in truth, he *was* a magician's familiar, and he likely wouldn't be in the way. Jamie wouldn't stand for that sort of nonsense.

"Lonely," Clint whined at me pitifully, as if sensing my internal debate.

I knew very well anyone in our apartment would have watched him in a heartbeat. He'd squirmed his way into all their hearts, Mrs. Henderson especially. It wasn't him I worried about. Jamie, on the other hand, still suffered from night terrors. She slept better with him at hand. I sensed he'd been brought along more for her sake than his.

In the end, I decided to trust her judgement. "I've no objection. Ladies, I believe you gathered everything I need for this. Shall we get on the road?"

McSparrin was obviously excited to work a murder outside our precinct, as she immediately loaded into the back. I attempted to do the same—surely the back was safer than the front—but Seaton beat me to the other seat. In the end, I was stuck in the front, where I could see the danger coming.

Well, perhaps she'd be more sedate with a full load of passengers and delicate equipment. Consideration for Clint's safety alone might make her slow down. Wouldn't it?

I saw the wicked gleam of anticipation in her dark brown eyes and groaned. No, of course I wouldn't be that lucky.

Report 02: Murder, Murder Most Foul

The car jostled along the highway at a speed one could only describe as maniacally insane. I bounced a little on the springs of the seat, a death grip on both the door and the back ridge of the bucket seats, and stared at the speedometer with rising panic.

How had she gotten the car to do *fifty miles an hour*?!

I knew she was a speed demon, but even Jamie couldn't surpass the mechanical restraints of an engine! How was she doing this?

Cars whirled past us in a blur of color. More than a few horns sounded, mostly out of alarm. Jamie wasn't anywhere close to them or in danger of collision. The wind whipped around us, scenting the car with freshly cut grass and sunshine, and it would have been a beautiful drive if I hadn't been in fear of my life.

Jamie was clearly enjoying herself, singing away at the top of her lungs: "The hills are alive with the sound of screaming~"

I of course didn't recognize the song, although the lyrics were unfortunately appropriate. I'd ask her about the song in its entirety later, assuming we survived the trip.

Seaton sat right behind her, so he must have seen the speedometer as well. He leaned forward and put his mouth next to Jamie's ear, raising his voice to be heard over the road noise. Even with the hard canopy top and windows, noise infiltrated the car, prohibiting casual conversation. "How are you doing fifty?!"

Jamie called back without turning her head, "Ellie and I worked on the engine! This is a souped-up version!"

Heavens preserve us, both women were going to get me killed with their tinkering. "Just because you CAN go that fast doesn't mean you should!"

"Look, Henri, I paid for the whole speedometer, so I'm going to *use* the whole speedometer."

The car skidded sideways, the roads slick from the rain we'd gotten last night. My heart, already trying to beat out of my chest, dropped into my stomach. I gave her a pleading look, begging her silently to not get us all killed.

Either she realized I was a breath away from heart failure, or common sense belatedly snuck a word in. Either way, she slowed, the car going down to a saner thirty miles. (I use the word saner with the utmost sarcasm.)

"The tires are definitely not gripping the road enough to continue," Jamie noted to her terrified passengers. "We'll have to work on the tires and suspension next. But I can tell Ellie the updates worked. We maintained that speed for a solid ten minutes."

And here it felt like ten years. I pried one finger loose at a time on each hand, pulling myself free of the death grip I'd maintained on the edge of the door. The dash and bucket seat offered nothing to cling to with their smooth surfaces. Clint had used his claws to maintain his position in the middle of the bucket seat, although he seemed to enjoy the speed.

Seeing my shaking hands, Clint came over to curl up in my lap, his delicate paw stroking my chest in a "there, there" manner. Which was patently absurd. I refused to be comforted by that. He purred at me, the ridiculous creature, and I found myself petting him without making the conscious decision to do so. Which, of course, only made him purr louder.

Seaton, still as unruffled as a clam, mentioned from the backseat, "I updated Queen Regina about our status. She's pleased we've made such good time. She also said no one else but the local constables and doctor have gone in."

"I've barely been given the basics." McSparrin's voice lilted upwards in question.

"We don't have much more than that," Seaton said darkly. "No more than what was reported to the queen, at any rate. Bit of a fluky over there at the moment."

"Bit of a what?" Jamie asked, baffled.

Now that we were going slower, it was easier to hear, and I managed to respond without shouting. "A fluky. It's a maritime term meaning a light wind that blows in every direction. It generally means there's a great deal of activity but nothing actually getting done."

"Ah." She gave me a nod of thanks for the definition. "I don't expect much help from the local police. This isn't their wheelhouse, and it's basically up to us to solve this one."

"Is that why I'm here?" McSparrin asked.

"In part," Jamie allowed, a quick smile gracing her features. "In part because I thought you'd like more experience investigating murders."

"You're right on both counts." McSparrin sounded infinitely pleased.

As she should be. It was always a boon when a more seasoned detective took a younger officer under their figurative wing. I didn't have the knack for that sort of tutoring, nor the right personality for it, but Jamie excelled at it. It was a blessing she did so. Truly, her knowledge was far more advanced than our current civilization. I referred not only to her knowledge of technology, but of criminal science as well. Once her writing skills were up to speed, I hoped to encourage her to write a thesis on everything she knew.

Sheffield lay far outside of Kingston, along the picturesque coastline that made up our eastern border. For the most part, we passed over flat country. Little better than moors, really. Poppies of all different colors covered the area, the road cutting a swath between the blooms, and it looked like something out of a painting. I found it a pity we were under a tight deadline and couldn't stop and linger for a moment. It was the right setting and scenery for a picnic. Assuming one could withstand the heat.

I saw signs of the recent storms that had razed the area as we got closer to the sea. What few trees grew in the area were upturned, their roots exposed to the sky. Two storms had hit within the past fortnight, the strong winds and tidal waves causing a great deal of havoc. "I read in the paper that a mother storm ravaged the coast recently. Did that hit Sheffield?"

"Oh yes," Seaton affirmed, and there was a sad note in his voice I couldn't explain. "Sheffield didn't take the brunt of it, but they were hard hit. Several trading ships were nearby, and they weren't able to get into safe harbor before the storm was upon them. Burtchell saved three of them before they were dashed against the cliffs."

"Wait, *our* Burtchell? Royal Mage Burtchell?" McSparrin demanded.

I twisted in my seat to see Seaton as well, just as surprised. I'd only caught part of the story in the newspaper. I'd not been aware of the connection to our victim.

Seaton gave a sad smile. "Yes. I realize he was retired, but his magic was as strong as ever, and he specialized in transportation magic. We were all proud of his quick thinking. I imagine the inhabitants of Sheffield will take this very hard, as their local hero has been murdered."

This anecdote raised more questions in my mind. The man might have been retired before his death, but clearly not without his magical prowess. Who had managed to kill him?

Jamie had little experience with this area of the country, so Seaton and I fell to navigating as we left the two-lane highway for the coastal road. It dipped and curved, the flat lands giving way to hills and sharp drop-offs to the left side, where the ocean crashed against the rocks. I thought about begging for my life, but fortunately my partner took even further pity and slowed down as she navigated the many winding curves of the road. I only thrice feared we'd fall into the ocean—rather better than I expected, with her behind the wheel.

The scent of brine and water was strong indeed by the time Sheffield came into view. The houses stretched along the coast, then further up the hills in a splendid rainbow of colors. Shops lined the main thoroughfare, quaint signs declaring their businesses, everything from a seamstress to a variety of restaurants. One hotel we passed showed a vacancy sign and looked more than acceptable, its three-story height standing tall and pristine among the backdrop of blue ocean. We might put up there while investigating. I did see damage to some of the buildings: signs of windows being broken, roofs under repair, even one deck roped off from being half-collapsed. The town had not come through that wave of storms unscathed.

"Looks like a pretty tourist town," Jamie commented.

"Yes, shame its image is spoiled by a gruesome murder, isn't it?" Seaton rejoined darkly. "Our plan, I take it, is to go straight to Burtchell's house?"

"I'd prefer to. I want to get an idea of what went down before we settle in here for the night." Jamie cast a look skyward, lips pursed in contemplation.

I did understand her concern. We were well into the afternoon at this juncture, leaving us precious little of the day left to work in. My stomach protested the absence of a midday repast. I consoled it with a pat and a promise of dessert after dinner. "Let's at least take a look at it, set Weber on the corpse and get his take on matters, then we can find a hotel and dinner."

My colleagues murmured agreements, no one objecting. Excellent.

Queen Regina had given us the house number, so we knew where to go. Not knowing the town so precisely, we did have to stop for directions, but Burtchell's house wasn't far from the main road. A little further up in the hills, it was a very nice bungalow overlooking the sea. I could see the appeal of retiring here. Or could, if the town had possessed more than four restaurants and a bookshop.

An officer stood outside the bungalow, waiting and guarding the place. He was a half-elf who appeared to be middle-aged, his greying mustache thick enough to cover his mouth. I could just detect his heritage in the pointed ears and the darker, ebony tone of his skin. The hat on his head sat low, obscuring his eyes, but he doffed it as we pulled into the gravel driveway. Stepping off the narrow porch, he gave us a greeting—and a doubletake at seeing two female officers. It was a rare thing, granted, and I hoped him not the type to discriminate unduly because of gender. I'd rather not scrape him off the ground after Jamie got through with him.

He visibly hesitated, not sure who to approach, then his eyes lit on Seaton with something like relief. Seaton's appearance was unmistakable. He dressed flamboyantly even in this weather. "RM Seaton?"

"That's me," Seaton answered forthrightly, coming forward with a hand outstretched. "Who might you be?"

"Constable Parmenter, sir. Thank you for coming so promptly. I don't mind telling you, this isn't something we want our noses in. Smacks of magic, it does."

My attention sharpened on him. I didn't always harken to such opinions, as the uneducated masses often attributed anything strange to magic. To them, no other explanation existed. Officers of the law, however, were educated in the broader sense of what magic could do. They were more likely to give credit where it was due.

"Constable, I am Doctor Henri Davenforth, Magical Examiner. This is my colleague, Detective Jamie Edwards—"

His deep-set eyes widened in recognition and he might have uttered a strangled, "Cor," although it was hard to tell.

"—and Officer Penny McSparrin," I finished somewhat wryly. Of course he recognized Jamie. Few officers did not. "Do you mind explaining your comment just now? What makes you think this 'smacks of magic'?"

To his credit, Parmenter recovered his composure promptly. "Pleasure to meet you all. Why don't you come inside, Doctor, and I'll walk you through it. See what you make of it."

That was fair enough, and in truth, what I preferred. I wanted to make my own judgements without his opinions clouding me. "Very well. Give me one moment."

I fetched my magical spectacles and a wand, wishing to not bumble into anything unduly. With those at the ready, Constable Parmenter led the way to the front door, narrating the scene as he went in a scratchy baritone. We all gathered close on his heels, Jamie with a notebook in hand, her pencil dancing along the page.

"—at the doctor's clinic, you say? Where exactly is that?"

"Ah, he's in town, on the main strip, across from the train station."

Seaton already had his texting pad out and wrote the direction down. I caught a glimpse of the recipient as I came to stand next to him. Of course. Weber. The coroner was behind us, thanks to Jamie's insane driving, and he wouldn't know where to go. Fortunately, Weber had a pad on him. He'd not need to needlessly stop at the station to get directions.

Parmenter seemed quite intrigued by the pad, but he asked no questions. He waited until Seaton was done, made sure he had all of our attention, then cleared his throat. "It's like this, sirs, ladies," Parmenter said as he gestured toward the door. "It was the housekeeper as found him. She came in at seven sharp, she says, and the door was locked. Had to let herself in with a key."

"Was that typical?" Jamie interrupted.

He blinked at her quite blankly. "I don't know, ma'am. She didn't think it odd, not when she was recounting herself to me."

That answer did not satisfy my partner, I could see that clearly. No doubt she'd ask that question again later. "Continue, Constable."

"Anyway, she comes in through the front, and finds the milk and cream sitting just inside. That she did find odd, what with the outer door being locked. But she gathered that up"—as he spoke, he pushed the front door open so we could see the vestibule inside—"and walked through here."

The vestibule was not large, more a tiled entryway with a single chair and a rack for shoes off to one side. It was a practical arrangement, a way for people to shed outerwear before entering into the house, and nothing more. I gestured to the door on the opposite side. "Was that also locked?"

"It was, sir. She said she opened it with a key as well, then went in, delivering the bottles of milk and cream to the kitchen. She then went for the front parlor, hoping to tidy it up before her employer woke and asked for breakfast."

We stepped through the second door and I took a moment to get my bearings. There was a cozy dining nook off to the left, the glimpse of a kitchen beyond it with a half-open door. To the right was the front parlor, with its semi-stiff furniture, knick-knacks on the mantel above a cold fireplace, and polished wood floors. It did look as if someone had been there the night before, as ashtrays with half-stubbed out cigarettes and one cigar littered the side tables.

"It was as she was moving towards the parlor that she saw something strange." Parmenter gestured to the open doorway further ahead, past the parlor. "She said she caught a glimpse of a man in the mirror. Not expecting her employer up this early, she went through to see who it was."

I could see how she might have caught a glimpse, as he put it. The mirror hung on the far wall, facing the doorway. I followed the constable through the door once more and into a private study. This space had the air of daily use. The back wall was covered completely in shelving, with every imaginable color and size of book on display. A desk sat off to the left, facing the window. Two chairs sat to the right, both matching red brocade, one in the middle of the room and the other in the corner.

"She found RM Burtchell in the corner chair," Parmenter relayed with a grimace on his wide face. "He had a hole dead center of his forehead, a letter in his hand. She went immediately for us, and we came up as quick as we dared. Doctor Avery—he's the only one in thirty miles of the town—did us the favor of carting him to his clinic. Said there wasn't anything to do for the poor blighter, but thought it better the body sit in a cold space while we waited on you."

"We appreciate his help," Seaton assured the constable. The man seemed in need of the reassurance as his worry eased. "Were you first on scene?"

"Yes, sir, I was."

"You said he had a letter in hand?" Jamie prompted, still taking notes in a quick hand. "Where is it?"

"On his desk, ma'am." Parmenter seemed a little in awe of my partner. Or perhaps in fear of her. He couldn't make himself meet her eyes, choosing instead to focus on anything else. "There were two pages in his hand; the other three had fallen to the ground."

"So he was reading the letter when he was killed." She tapped her pencil to her mouth, thinking hard.

As she fetched the letter from the desk, McSparrin pointed to the chair in the middle of the room. "That doesn't look like it normally sits there. It's an odd placement, to be right in the middle of the room like that."

It was an excellent point, and one I'd been on the verge of making myself. "Quite so. I would imagine it would sit on the other side of the windows, flanking its twin. This placement suggests he had a guest, someone who had drawn the chair up to face him as they conversed."

"Someone he had to be very comfortable with, to open his mail in front of." McSparrin made her own notes, her cornflower blue eyes narrowed in thought.

"Constable." Seaton looked steadily around the room, his nose flaring like a hunting dog's. "You said you suspected magic. There's a great deal of it here, not unexpectedly, but I'm not sensing anything in particular that would incline me to believe magic was used in this case."

"It's not so much that, sir, as the wound. There's a large hole in RM Burtchell's head, but we've no bullet casing or even a gun on site," Parmenter explained. "We looked about the yard as well, but there's no weapon to be found that would match the wound."

Ah. Now that made more sense of his assumption. It also made it clear what we needed to do first. "Seaton, if you'll do a seeking spell for the murder weapon? I wish to examine those two doors, see if someone locked it magically behind them."

He agreed with a single nod. I turned on my heel and went back to the front doors, using a diagnostic spell on both interior and exterior locks. There was a great deal of magic prevalent in the house which, really, wasn't unexpected. A magician of his caliber would naturally use magic throughout his day, and that had permeated into the very walls of this house. That didn't even take into consideration the warding spell over the house. Still, I could find no sign the locks had been magically manipulated.

Jamie drifted up to stand behind me, watching curiously. "How is it?"

"I cannot detect any forced entry on this door. Nor any magical manipulation of it."

"I just took a quick look around the bottom floor. There's no other door."

I found that odd and straightened to give her a look askance. "Wouldn't there normally be a back door?"

"You'd think, right? But the house abuts the back of the hill at such a steep angle that there's no room for a door. That's why the housekeeper came through the front, I betcha. She didn't have any other door to use. I need to check all the upstairs windows. Maybe our killer got out that way?"

"To what purpose?" I countered. "To make this seem a suicide?"

"Possibly? If that was the attempt, it failed. Not one person has even suggested suicide so far." She looked downright gleeful, practically bouncing in place. "I do love a good locked room mystery."

"It seems we have one on hand."

"I'm going to get Clint up on the roof, see if he can spot anything strange up there. See if you can find Burtchell's keys while you're down here. I've only got the housekeeper's set. Surely Burtchell had one of his own." As she spoke, she slipped past me, heading out the door. "Let's find the postman, housekeeper, and milkman after this."

I followed one part of that, but not the other. "Why the postman? You think the letter was delivered this morning?"

She paused in the outer door and waggled her hand back and forth. "Maybe this morning, maybe yesterday. I want to know, hence why we need to ask."

"Fair enough. After we find those three and interview them, I think we should stop for the day. We'll need Weber's report before truly knowing how Burtchell was killed."

"And dinner. I don't know about you, but I'm starving."

I was so glad to hear her say that. "Yes, I'm quite famished."

She nodded agreement and stepped out completely. I could hear her calling as she went, "Clint? Stop chasing butterflies. I need you to skulk on the roof for me."

McSparrin approached with a faint frown on her face. "Jamie's going up with Clint on the roof, she said. I can—" She cut off as singing started and thumps sounded on the roof.

"Everybody wants to be a cat," Clint sang, and there was a mischievous, smug tone in his voice. "Because a cat's the only cat who knows where it's at~"

"I regret teaching you *Aristocats*," Jamie grumbled loudly from the front door. "Stop preening and help me, you furball."

Wryly, McSparrin finished, "I can investigate the windows upstairs, see if the killer went out that way."

"Actually, see if you can find Burtchell's set of keys," I requested, smiling up towards the ceiling. What were those two even doing out there? There was far too much stomping about and singing for them to be checking for points of entry. "I'll need to check the windows to see if any of them had spellwork in place. You're frowning, McSparrin."

"Yes," she agreed, the furrows between her brows deepening. "Just thinking...it really does seem like one of those locked room mysteries you read in the novels. And I don't think that's what Queen Regina wants to hear just now."

Stonking deities. It had quite escaped me we'd need to update our impatient queen soon. "Fortunately, that's Seaton's job."

"I heard that!" Seaton called from the study. "May I remind you our illustrious queen went to Jamie? Not me."

"You make an excellent point, old chap," I called back. "We'll have her do it."

"As long as it isn't me," McSparrin muttered.

My sentiment exactly.

Jamie called from outside, "Could you help me with something, Henri?"

"What might that be?" I called back. I knew from her tone she was teasing and didn't really need my presence.

"This knife in my back—I can't seem to reach it!"

Oh ha, ha.

What was the song you sang earlier?

Ah, it's from a movie. I changed the lyrics a bit, but it's from

THE SOUND OF MUSIC.

And there's lots of screaming?

lol no, that lyric change is courtesy of my highschool English teacher.

To be honest, I don't remember the real lyrics anymore.

Report 03: Bullets and Bouillabaisse

I'm still confused by this notion of putting a hashtag in front of the word.

Hashtags 101. Round two. Begin!

The housekeeper, Mrs. Landry, was nearly insensible with shock. Tears kept escaping the sides of her eyes, trailing down her round cheeks, and she dabbed at them constantly with a handkerchief. She sat in the front parlor of her house, wearing a plain white dress for mourning. I had the sense to stand back and allow McSparrin and Jamie to do the questioning. It would be easier for them to approach her. I sat on the far side of the room with Seaton and took notes.

Jamie leaned forward in her chair, smile kind. "Mrs. Landry, I know you've had a terrible morning. I don't want to pester you, but I'd like to find out who killed your employer."

Mrs. Landry sniffed, tears coming afresh. "As to that, Detective, I want him found. RM Burtchell, he was a sweet man. Always a kind word for me, and he didn't put on airs of him being better than any of us. There's no cause for someone to kill him."

"I promise, we'll do everything in our power to find him. I just need more information than I have. Can you walk me through a few things? I have no idea who his associates were, you see."

"Of course, Detective, you ask. I'll do my best to answer."

"Thank you. First, walk me through this morning. What time did you get in?"

"Seven, same as always. RM Burtchell, he liked to have breakfast about half past. Sometimes he was coming in from a late night, sometimes he just chose to get up early, but he always broke his fast at the same time."

Jamie's eyebrows arched in question. "Late night? Did he stay out often?"

"Oh, he loved to play cards with the other gentlemen," Mrs. Landry responded with a watery smile. "Sometimes he hosted it at his own house, sometimes he went to a friend's. They rotated on who hosted, you see. They played for laughs, he said. I think sometimes money did get involved, but not usually."

"Was last night a late night for him?"

She hesitated strongly. "It's hard to tell...that is, I never knew until I asked. He'd sometimes stumble in at the crack of dawn. The moment he was home, he'd change into pajamas and a robe, and he was like that this morning. He'd gotten the paper, too, I saw that. He always read the paper over breakfast, checked the races."

"So you can't tell either way. I understand. If I wanted to answer that question, who could I ask?"

"Mr. Walterson or Mr. Villarreal would be able to tell you. If there was a game going on, they were always playing."

I made note of both names.

"So you came in at seven," Jamie picked back up to her original point smoothly. "And then what?"

"Well, as I told the constables, I unlocked the front door with my key. I found the milk and cream inside, which I thought odd, what with the door being locked. But I picked up both bottles, then found the inner door locked too. I had to put them down to unlock it."

"Was that unusual? To have both doors locked?"

"No, not really. The wards were set to engage fully when both doors were locked."

Seaton stepped forward from where he'd been hovering by my chair, catching the housekeeper's attention. "Dear lady, I must ask a few questions about that. The wards showed daily use. Did Burtchell normally keep the doors locked at all times?"

"More or less, sir," she answered with a deferential nod of the head. "He said there were papers and things inside he didn't want anyone getting hold of. He was doing magical research. He tried to explain it to me once, but it went mostly over my head. But he was very adamant the wards stay up unless we had a guest coming in."

It made sense, of course. Putting up and taking down wards on a constant basis would be draining, even for a royal mage. Why not tie them to a simple action? It would allow him to have guests and an employee without constantly working the wards. Tying them to the locks on both doors was a neat solution.

Or should have been. With the wards fully up, how did the murderer get inside?

Jamie took up the questioning once more. "The wards were up, then, when you came in. It's why you didn't think anything was wrong at first?"

"Yes. Because what could get past a royal mage's wards? I didn't realize he'd been…he'd been…" She cut off on a sob, folding in on herself.

McSparrin left her chair to put an arm around those shaking shoulders, soothing her. "Shh, it's alright."

Jamie grasped the woman's hand firmly. "I'm sorry, Mrs. Landry. I just have two more questions for now. Then I'll let you rest. RM Burtchell, did he smoke?"

Wiping at her eyes, Mrs. Landry managed a nod.

"Cigars, cigarettes? Both?"

"Cigars," she whispered hoarsely. "Only cigars. He didn't like the taste of cigarettes."

Oh? Interesting. We'd found the remains of both in the ashtray in the study.

"And do you know of anyone who was angry with him? Anyone who might have wished him harm?"

Mrs. Landry immediately shook her head. "No. No, he was a kind man. A good man. A bit fond of the cards, maybe, but every man has one vice, doesn't he just. And the people in Sheffield, we all adored him. He was a hero, you know. Saved three ships from capsizing in that horrible storm a fortnight ago. I don't understand why anyone would want him dead."

Yes, that was indeed the question. I wrote down the word *gambling* in my notes with a question mark. Was he in financial trouble? I couldn't imagine it, that a man of his standing would be in dire financial straits, but people sometimes fell down that hole of avarice to absolute ruin. Or had someone been after his research, whatever that was?

We thanked her for her time, then left. As we exited the quaint house, I looked at the sky again and frowned. Time had certainly gotten away from us. It was edging towards sunset now, the air growing colder as it swept in from the ocean. The sky was brushed with gold, reds, oranges, and purple clouds in a painter's display of colors. Quite pretty, really.

"Red sky at night, sailor's delight," Seaton observed, his face also turned towards the horizon. "Also our sign to stop for the night and find a hotel, I think."

"And dinner," McSparrin implored. "I'm half-wasted away."

"We all are," I assured her as my stomach rumbled threateningly. "Let's do so promptly. I'll message Weber to meet us at the nearest restaurant. Perhaps we can exchange notes over dinner."

We chose the hotel I'd made note of on the way in. It was not only impressively clean but quite reasonable in price. The ladies got the best rooms in the house, as their windows faced the sea, which Seaton teasingly bemoaned. Since the hotel had a restaurant in the main dining hall, we chose to try our luck with it.

As we entered the carpeted dining room, I spied Weber already there, still dressed in his suit, which inclined me to believe he had not had a chance to perform the autopsy yet. He'd chosen a table in the center of the room, more by happenstance than design, as most of the tables were full even at this hour of the evening. The patronage promised the food would, at least, be more than edible.

"Hello," he greeted us as we settled around the table. Its snowy tablecloth was already covered in place settings, as well as an appetizer of cheese dip and sliced bread in the center. I exercised great restraint to not fall upon the offering like a starving wolf.

"Weber, you delightful man," Seaton returned, eagerly reaching for the appetizer. "Tell me you've already ordered for all of us."

"Of course I did. You think I'm a fool? We all missed lunch, and Davenforth's love of food is legendary. I took no chances. They had a special tonight for bouillabaisse, cheddar mashed potatoes, and asparagus with cheese and garlic biscuits. I didn't think anyone would object to that."

Jamie already had a mouthful of bread and cheese dip and spoke behind her hand. "Good call."

I didn't chide her for the lack of manners. I was a mere breath away from exhibiting the same behavior.

We didn't speak until the appetizer was gone. It barely made a dent in the hollow feeling of my stomach and in an effort to distract myself, I sipped at my chilled water and inquired, "Weber, did you have a chance to do an examination?"

"Only a cursory one. I want to take a proper look tomorrow, when I have more time. I did speak with the doctor, Avery. Nice chap. Said he'd seen RM Burtchell for years because of his heart condition. It wasn't too unmanageable, according to him, just something that acted up under highly stressful situations or due to extreme exercise."

Seaton snorted. "Hence why he'd retired. A royal mage is under constant stress and we always end up running about like headless chickens."

Weber flashed him a small smile and shrug. "You'd know. At any rate, he had another good fifteen years of life left, according to the doctor. No danger of him dying anytime soon. I will say this. The body struck me as...odd. Dr. Avery thought the man had been shot in the head, and I admit, the hole has the right size and general shape for a bullet. But I didn't find one in his head."

Jamie's head came up like a bloodhound that had possibly caught onto the right scent. "Exit wound?"

"Clear to the back in a straight line."

"Same size?" she pressed. "The exit wound on the back of the skull wasn't any larger?"

Weber turned toward her, his focus sharp and intrigued. "No, not any larger. Exactly the same size. Does that mean something to you?"

Her lips pursed thoughtfully. "It might. Weber, any sign of gun powder?"

"Not a trace. Which I found odd, frankly."

"I wasn't able to locate a weapon of any sort on the premises, even with seeking spells," Seaton tacked on, expression screwed up in a grimace, "So I share your disgruntlement on the lack of evidence. Anything else of interest, Doctor Weber?"

Weber shrugged as if he wasn't sure what to add. "With the force of the impact, I would say the attack came from perhaps five feet away? Or a little further. Certainly no closer."

"So definitely not a suicide." Seaton looked relieved to hear this.

"Not even a possibility," Weber assured him. "Why,

was that in question?"

"A remote one," Jamie answered absently. I could see the cogs turning in her mind. "Both front doors were locked, and there were no other doors to the house. The windows were all locked as well, and the wards were up. The two sets of keys we know of are both accounted for—Burtchell's were in his desk, and the landlady had the other set. We can't figure out how the murderer got in."

"Portation spell of some sort?" Weber offered.

Seaton and I both shook our heads in tandem. I explained patiently, "The wards prevented portation spells. Also lock-picking, damage to the property, and so forth. It would have taken a considerable amount of physical or magical force to break through the wards, and we'd certainly see the damage."

"Ah. Well, it was a thought. I grant you, those kinds of protections would be expected around a mage's property." Weber looked hopefully at Jamie. "Have you seen a wound like this before?"

"Only once." She paused and looked around the table, finding us all ears. "This is a bit gruesome to talk about before dinner."

"Don't stop now," McSparrin complained. "Besides, we're all policemen."

Seaton snorted. "I beg your pardon."

She waved a hand at him. "You investigate things all the time, you're basically like us."

McSparrin did rather have a point. He must have seen that, as he shrugged assent.

Seeing that none of us were discomfited with the topic, Jamie continued. "Alright, I'm not sure how much you know about bullet wounds through a head, so I'll go over the basics. If someone is shot, the bullet will make a neat hole through the front, but a rather large exit wound in the back as it loses its velocity. The bullet becomes misshapen as it travels through bone and brain. A small enough caliber doesn't go all the way through, and will instead be stuck inside the brain matter. If there is an exit wound of the same size as the entry, that means the bullet was moving at extremely high velocity. More velocity than a regular handgun could offer."

Weber frowned thoughtfully, his eyes focused on some internal vision. "Are we looking for something other than a bullet? The size and shape is right for the wound. I can't think of anything that would make the same wound so neatly."

I was equally perplexed. "Perhaps we need to locate the bullet. If there was one, and it moved at such high velocity, it surely would have ended up in the wall behind his head, would it not?"

Jamie gave me a nod. "That's my guess. We didn't look for it today, but then, we didn't think to, either. Sherard couldn't find any weapon in the house. Let's do that first thing in the morning. If it wasn't a bullet, then we need to find the murder weapon. Well, we need to find the murder weapon regardless."

"And a motive, and witnesses, and a murderer," Seaton rejoined in dark humor. "Quite a few things for us to find. Have you updated Queen Regina yet?"

Jamie made a face. "Isn't that your job?"

"My dear, might I remind you that when this went down, it was *you* she immediately went to? That makes you in charge of this case."

She groaned, shoulders slumping. "Of course it does. Alright, fine. You and I both can report in to her after dinner."

Seaton looked ready to object, only to close his mouth again. No doubt he'd remembered Jamie's vocabulary wasn't up to snuff yet. She'd need someone to sit with her to translate anything she didn't know.

Our dinner arrived and we ate it with much gusto. It was splendid fare, the soup lovely, the vegetables seasoned just how I liked, and the biscuits still steaming from the oven. I ordered a chocolate monstrosity to cleanse my palate and wasn't in the least surprised when Jamie stole several forkfuls. I do believe if she were denied chocolate, she'd expire on the spot.

We received more than a few looks—some bemused, others knowing—as Jamie forthrightly helped herself to my dessert. I put most of her behavior down to her utter tenacity where chocolate was concerned and didn't think anything more of it. No doubt I'd get ribbed by Seaton later, though.

We went our own directions after dinner. I chose to walk onto the back balcony of the hotel to stretch my legs a bit and enjoy the sea air. It was cleaner and cooler here, but we were also north of Kingston. The wind off the sea took the edge off the heat in a pleasant manner and I stood there for a while with my face towards the evening breeze, enjoying it. It had been a largely stressful day and I liked the chance to unwind before retiring.

"Henri."

I turned my head to spot Clint sauntering toward me. I say sauntering with considerable disbelief, because while he looked utterly relaxed in his gait, he was balancing upon a four-inch-wide balustrade. That overhung a sheer drop into the ocean. It was one thing for me to lean my elbows upon it, quite another to watch him walk as if his very life didn't depend on his surefootedness.

"Clint, for magic's sake, why are you walking on the handrail?"

He blinked at me as if he didn't understand the point of my inquiry.

I swear, he did things of that nature to cause me heart failure. He was far too much like his owner in this aspect. "Come here. I'll take you to Jamie."

That offer was agreeable to him and he leapt

lightly onto my chest, his front paws balancing over my shoulder. I wrapped both hands securely around him, feeling better for it, and immediately put distance between us and the ocean below. "Were you fed? Would you like some water?"

"Jamie gave water." He settled in, his chin on my shoulder, and purred. "Warm."

"Yes, I suppose I am. Is that what you were doing? Looking for warmth?" His logic was entirely inscrutable, even on the best of days.

"Bored. Lonely."

"So you were exploring. I see. Well, she's speaking with the queen now. I've no doubt you can curl up in her lap for a while."

He pulled himself up enough to rub his cheek against mine, his fur catching on my stubble. "Nice Henri."

Despite myself, I grinned. "It's a good thing you're charming. Even if you and your master are both intent on scaring me to death."

Jamie's Additional Report 3.5

The way Sherard was acting worried me a little. I'd rarely seen him so down in spirits. He'd escaped from our conference call with Queen Regina so quickly I didn't get a chance to ask him anything. But as I passed his room, on the way back from the bathroom, I saw the light still on under the door. If he was still up, I'd take the chance for a little one-on-one with him. I knocked on Sherard's door with a cat cradled in my arm, as Clint was worried about our friend too.

"Enter!" he called out.

The door gave way easily under my hand as I pushed inside. Sherard was seated on the foot of the bed, just in shirt sleeves and pants, and he honestly looked a little rough. Usually he was so carefree I thought of him as an adult Energizer Bunny. I wasn't quite sure why he was taking this case harder than usual. "Hey. You okay?"

He patted the bed next to him and I took the invitation to sit next to him. Clint sprawled out over our laps as I settled, Sherard's head leaning against the top of mine as he absently rubbed at the cat's ears. "I knew him."

Uh-oh. "You knew Burtchell?"

A deep, weary sigh slipped from his throat. "It was his position I took over. Burtchell stayed three months to help mentor me before he fully retired. He was a friend. He was one of those wacky, insane people who thought up brilliant things because he just didn't see the world like anyone else." A reminiscent smile slipped over his face, his mind going back to a happier moment. "When I first met him, he was in a very heated argument with the other two royal mages about the proper way to tackle the pigeon population. They're slowly taking over the city, it's still something of an issue. Little better than flying rats, really. His solution was to create a creature—much like Clint here—but with wings. Something that could fly, and shoot fire, and decimate pigeon nests."

Fly, shoot fire, and...no way. "He wanted to create dragons?!"

Sherard chuckled. "So, you've heard of them on Earth as well?"

"In mythology, no one's got proof they ever actually existed," I explained rapidly, still indignant. "He wanted to create dragons and *you stopped him?* What's wrong with you!"

That got him to laugh, a full-out belly laugh. "I didn't stop him, you know. I thought it a rather good method. But this is part of the reason why I like you so much. You remind me so much of him—you don't think along the same lines either."

I was still a little pissed. The chance of dragons. Gone. "I'll accept the compliment."

"As you should. But that's how Burtchell was, always proposing some outlandish thing, and the odd thing was, the majority of the time it was a workable solution. I adored the three months I worked alongside him. Magic was *fun* with him. I didn't see him much after he moved out here, but we stayed in fairly consistent contact. He was one of the people assigned to help sift through Belladonna's work."

So this man was a colleague, a friend, something of a mentor...no wonder Sherard was taking this hard. "Ah, man, I'm so sorry. I didn't realize he was a friend."

"I don't think I really mentioned him much to you. We have a habit of not talking about Belladonna in front of you."

For good reason, granted. It wasn't like I was really receptive to talking about her. "Yeah. If this is too hard for you—"

He shook his head, the motion gentle against my own. "No. I volunteered to come. I want to help catch who did this. And the worst thing, the part I was worried most about, didn't occur. I wasn't sure if I could stomach seeing his body."

Ah. I internally winced. Yeah, most people didn't handle

that well. Fortunately, at least for my friend, Burtchell had already been removed. I personally would have preferred to see the way the body was arranged in the chair. We were slim on clues as it was. Still, I couldn't begrudge Sherard the silver lining. "If you're sure. But if you change your mind, you tell me, okay? Don't push yourself."

He snorted, as if I'd just said something amusing. "You push yourself all the time."

"Yes, but I like putting myself just outside of my comfort zone. And I'm crazy."

Sherard put an arm around my waist and hugged me to him. "That you are. The best kind of crazy."

I sensed that right then, he didn't really need words. He just needed a friend. I could give him silence and time, if that's all he needed. We sat side by side, petting a cat, and let time march on for a while.

Report 04: Unanswered Questions

The beds were a touch too firm for my liking, but the sheets were fresh and the pillows soft. I slept relatively well and rose feeling refreshed and ready to tackle our mystery anew. The bathroom off my room was quite modern, and I saw at least one of Jamie's inventions: the temperature dial on the tub faucet regulating the hot water.

Whenever I saw something of her design, it always made me extraordinarily proud. She often deflected compliments of her inventions, stating she wasn't actually inventing anything, just copying things from home. But I knew simply using an item didn't give you any sense of how it operated. She'd either learned how it functioned on her world, or had the intelligence to sort it out here with Ellie Warner. Either way, it demanded excellent recall and cleverness. I would not be dissuaded from my compliments.

I went about my morning ablutions, readying myself for the day, then left the room in search of breakfast and my team. As I went down the stairs, I glanced out the tall, picturesque windows to see a stunning view of the sun glinting off the ocean waves, made all the better with the height I stood at. The hotel had been built on the side of a cliff, and its prominence made for excellent views.

Pausing on the landing, I caught sight of a figure running along the cliff edge, with something small and purple at her feet. I knew without needing to strain my eyes who it was—Jamie. Only she seemed intent on jogging in the mornings, no matter our location.

Shaking my head, I continued downstairs, fetching

a coffee for myself and a tall glass of iced water. Stepping out the side door of the hotel, I waited in the shade of the building, sipping on the excellent brew and watching as my partner slowed to a walk, cooling after her run. She'd apparently planned on jogging out here, as she wore her sweats and loose shirt, those tennis shoes she liked so much on her feet. I wouldn't have thought to pack in order to exercise while out on a case, but then, I didn't plan to exercise. Ever.

"Morning," she called out to me, still some distance away.

"Good morning," I returned. Holding up the glass, I offered, "Something cool?"

"Yes, thank you." Jamie's volume lowered as she came in closer.

Clint sashayed at her side, bright-eyed although not panting from the run. I knew he often ran with her, enjoying both the exercise and company, although he wasn't sure what the point of it was. To the Felix, you ran when there was something to chase. I must say, I heartily agreed with that viewpoint. Running pointlessly along the streets seemed detrimental to the soul, even if it supposedly improved the waistline.

Still, it was readily apparent she enjoyed her runs—flushed from the exercise, perky and alert, smiling from ear to ear with satisfaction. Her pleasure widened as she accepted the cold glass from my hand.

"Ever thoughtful," she teased before quaffing half the glass.

I cleared my throat, knowing she was teasing but unsure how to gracefully accept the praise. "I admit I didn't anticipate you'd jog out here. You don't know the area well enough for it."

"I ran partially to learn the area better," she admitted, tongue darting out to capture a trace of water from her lips. "The area up here is so open, there's not many trees, and the houses aren't all that close together. I would think it'd be easy to see people coming and going."

"Yes, I'd noticed that myself." Belatedly, I looked down at Clint. "I didn't think to grab you water."

"I'm good," he said.

"He doesn't like to drink anything while he's hot, for some reason," Jamie explained. "And he's definitely hot. He's run a good four times the amount I have this—whoop, squirrel."

Clint took off like a shot, his body streamlined toward the ground as he sprinted smoothly across the manicured lawn and into the bushes hedging the side of the hotel. We heard a great deal of rustling as he tore through the foliage, a high-pitched squeak, and then a flurry of activity moving towards the front porch.

I was startled at this abrupt chase. "Does he do that often?"

"Most of the time we're jogging, really. He'll dart out to the side, catch something rodenty, and then come back to me all smug and satisfied. He'd be a good jogging buddy if he weren't so distractible." Shrugging, she went back to drinking her water.

But he kept her company and smiling, which was what I'd intended for him to do when I first acquired him. That satisfied me. "Did you see anything interesting while you were out?"

"Mmm, not so much see, but heard. I crossed paths with both the milkman and the postman. I don't think either believed me to be a detective"—a sweep of her hand indicated her ponytail and attire, and indeed she did not at all look the part—"but they answered my questions regardless. The milkman reported the front door was unlocked when he made his delivery. He opened the door and set both bottles just inside."

"Hence why they were inside the vestibule when Mrs. Landry arrived." Interesting. I made mental note of this, adding it to my timeline. "What time was this?"

"Half past six, or thereabouts. He wasn't sure exactly. It was more an estimate considering how long it takes for him to do his rounds."

I couldn't imagine the man would consult a watch while doing his job, so this was likely the best answer we were going to get. "And the postman?"

"Came in after, as he remembered seeing the bottles of cream and milk. He also put the mail just inside the vestibule, on the chair, he said, and rang the doorbell twice to alert Burtchell the mail was in. Now, he said something interesting. He heard two male voices inside the house. He didn't see who, and of course he wouldn't if he didn't take more than a step inside the house."

No, the vestibule was not open to the rest of the main floor. The walls would have prevented any line of sight. "But Burtchell had a visitor. Interesting. No idea who?"

Jamie's shoulders lifted in an elaborate shrug. "They sounded friendly, was all he remembered. He didn't linger to eavesdrop, just dropped the mail off and left again."

I sipped at my cooling coffee and considered the facts. "So, sometime between the mail being delivered and Mrs. Landry arriving, the doors were locked, and Burtchell murdered. What are the odds our postman actually heard the murderer?"

"I'd give it fifty-fifty at this point. Interesting thing to note, the men were smoking. Postman is a werewolf so I trust his nose on this, and he said he smelled both cigar and cigarette smoke."

"Which means that man, whoever he was, stayed long enough to smoke the cigarette. Even if he's not our suspect, he's likely the last one to see Burtchell alive. We need to find him, somehow."

"This is one of those times I wish you guys had DNA forensic ability," Jamie whined to me, head hanging for a moment. "It would make life so much easier."

She'd mentioned this to me before, on another case, although in truth I didn't understand the precise nuances of it. She'd explained it as something rather like a biological fingerprint, and I did think it would be brilliant if we could link such evidence together. Sadly, it would take either a significant advancement in either magic or science to do so. Perhaps Seaton and I should put our heads together, in between the dozen other projects we were already committed to.

How did Jamie put it? 'I'll sleep when I'm dead.' That was it.

"This DNA would help here, you think? But there's no blood on the butts."

"Not blood. Saliva," she explained. "Every cell of a body has DNA in it, and it can all be used to match up with the person in question. Saliva isn't an exception. If we were on Earth, I could take the saliva left on the butts and have it analyzed, then match it up with a DNA database—ah, records on file. It would help lead me to the killer. Well, assuming his DNA is on file. That's usually only in the case of past criminal activity, either criminal or victim. Still, you'd be surprised how often we get a hit."

I followed this closely. Often Jamie assumed something wasn't feasible or available in this world because our level of technology hadn't caught up yet. But sometimes her descriptions led me into insights, ways I could adapt these procedures in a magical way. Jamie was very much a logical thinker, heavily based in the sciences. Magical solutions didn't occur to her. (Which I found particularly amusing, since she's a famous witch killer.)

I had no immediate thoughts of how to adapt her world's technology in this case, but if I slept on it and gave my subconscious mind time to ruminate on the idea, perhaps I'd think of something later.

"Unfortunately, we'll have to do this another way. Shall I order you breakfast while you wash up?"

"Yes, please. Nothing seafood, anything else will be good."

I gave her an amused study. "When are you going to overcome your aversion to seafood for breakfast?"

"There is something fundamentally wrong with having fish at this hour of the morning," she shot back, passing me. "I won't be convinced otherwise."

Chuckling, I let her go.

Knowing women could take time to ready themselves, I finished my coffee before re-entering the hotel. As I made my way into the main dining room, I spied both Seaton and McSparrin already seated at a table, tucked into a fine breakfast of kippers, eggs, and toast. I spied a sidebar of dishes set out on warming plates as I passed it. So, they served a complimentary breakfast? Excellent, that saved us the time of ordering. I fetched a plate and loaded it with my own selection before joining my colleagues at the table.

"Morning," McSparrin greeted as I sat down. "You seen Weber or Jamie yet?"

"Jamie, yes. She's just come in from a morning jog and should be with us presently. Weber I've not seen hide nor hair of."

"Likely went to get an early start on things," Seaton offered before picking up his tea. "He mentioned last night he'd like to be back in Kingsport by this evening. He wasn't sure if he'd have enough time, as he wanted to be quite thorough in the autopsy."

"Ah. I admit it's a sensible plan, assuming he can do the autopsy that quickly." I trusted Weber to do the job thoroughly no matter what time constraints he might be under. He was methodical in that respect. Picking up a fork, I added, "I believe before we truly get this investigation underway, we need to find a room to use."

Somehow, working on a case inevitably meant writing out timelines on a board, gathering evidence to one location, and interviewing witnesses more than once. The other two immediately understood my point.

"I'll check with the station here," McSparrin offered. "Although I wouldn't hold my breath. We passed it yesterday, coming here, and it looked like it was made up of three rooms altogether, including the holding cells."

"Yes, that was my impression as well," Seaton confirmed. He had a thoughtful look on his face as his turned, panning the hotel dining room. "I wonder if they'd have a room here we could turn to the purpose?"

"Perhaps? Would you like to inquire?"

Seaton immediately dipped his head in agreement. "I will. I'm nearly done eating anyway."

I felt it only fair to warn them as I cut into my pork chop, "Jamie did speak with both postman and milkman while on her run. We have a tighter timeline to go off of, and the mystery of why the milk was inside the house is at least solved."

"I'll have her catch me up. Eat. I'll go see about a room."

"Seaton, there's a lead I wish to follow up on. People have mentioned to us that Burtchell was doing some magical research of some nature."

"Yes, I want to look into that. I didn't see any signs of magical research at first pass in the house. Let's investigate that." Seaton gave me a nod, then stood and headed for a hotel employee, easy to spot in the pure black uniforms the women wore.

The scent from the eggs, hash, pork chops, and biscuits was too alluring to ignore any further. I ate with gusto and no little enthusiasm, as being on a case with Jamie had taught me meals were happenstance at the best of times. She did like to eat, and made sure to do so in the mornings and evenings, but the middle of the day? Well, that was a bit of a wash.

Remembering my manners somewhat belatedly, I inquired of McSparrin, "Did you sleep well?"

"I did, sir, thanks for asking. I left my window open. The sea breeze was nice." She looked rather young in that moment, despite her blonde hair being up in a sensible bun, her uniform starchily pressed. "And you, Doctor?"

"Quite well, thank you for asking. I think this hotel was rather a good choice on our part."

"Fortunately," she agreed, expression growing sardonic. "Looks like this might take a while to solve."

I was not wholly displeased by being here but still, the thought of Sanderson being left in charge in my absence...it made me shudder. "Hopefully not too long. I expect when the news gets out of Sheffield that a royal mage has been murdered, the reporters will descend here in droves."

"Bite your tongue," Jamie growled, coming toward the table. She looked resplendent in a light linen suit, the style reminiscent of a man's day suit, but obviously tailored to her feminine form. With her hair in a braid, she looked every inch the professional detective. It was an interesting visual juxtaposition from the sweaty woman who had run around Sheffield this morning. "I do not want to deal with reporters."

"My dear friend, none of us do. But turning a blind eye to the possibility will not help us. Better to come up with a statement now to give them."

She grimaced again, as if biting into something foul, and sat with more aplomb than grace. "You're likely right. Anyone seen Clint?"

"He's still chasing whatever-it-is outside, I believe."

Shaking her head, she chose to eat. Sensible, really. Clint wasn't a dumb creature that needed to be led around by the nose. He'd turn up in his own good time.

Seaton rejoined us at the table with a satisfied expression. "The hotel manager has kindly given us a conference room here on the ground floor. It's the second door on the left, just off the main entrance. She's adamant we can have it as long as we need it, and free of charge. She told me she knew Burtchell personally, that he sometimes hosted parties or card games here, and she wants to help catch his killer in any way she can."

Jamie's head came up sharply. "Can she give us a list of his known associates?"

Tapping a finger along the side of his nose, Seaton assured her, "Already thought of that and asked. She promises us a list by the end of the day. It was rather news to me that Burtchell isn't the only famous person who's retired here. Apparently there're a number of people here I know, by reputation at least. She said he was friendly with most of them."

This news cheered me. "I do love a good suspect pool. Any tensions?"

"No, not that she knew of. And frankly I'd be surprised to hear it. He was a very easy-going sort, not the type to hold grudges."

Seaton idly toyed with his tea cup, turning it round and round in its saucer as he frowned down into its milky depths. He was the only one at the table who didn't look well rested, his normal makeup accents around his eyes absent, his dark hair not as perfectly combed into place. He also looked...strained. Sad. Of course, Burtchell was not unknown to him. I kicked myself for not realizing that to us, this was a case, but to Seaton, this was a friend brutally murdered. Of course he'd be grieving.

"While I was jogging, I saw the remains of the ships still on the rocks." Jamie looked thoughtful as she glanced around the table. "I heard from the locals, again, about how glad they were he was here, how they'd have lost all the ships if not for his interference. How they only lost two crews because of him that night. There's a great deal of mourning for him, like they've lost a local hero."

Seaton's expression turned dark and troubled. "I really don't understand this. No one seems to have any motive for killing him. And indeed, it would have to be quite a surprise. A mage of his caliber should have been able to thwart any attack."

That was the point that bothered me as well. Even at point blank range—and Weber seemed to think the attack fit within that spectrum—Burtchell should have been able to fight back, at least. His magic was not diminished because of his health. Why hadn't he?

What were we missing?

Report 05: A Study in Bullets

In the interest of efficiency, we divided duties, each to our own strengths. Jamie and McSparrin went to find who might have been with Burtchell yesterday morning. Seaton and I caught a ride with one of the constables and returned to Burtchell's bungalow. I say bungalow in the loosest concept of the term, as it had three bedrooms and sat two stories tall. It wasn't the grandest house on this street, and certainly not in the town, although I wasn't sure why. Burtchell was not particularly known for modesty. Unless he'd chosen the house because of its location? He had the best view of the sea from here.

The doors were locked, the wards still thrumming in a subdued manner, not showing any signs of distress. Thanking the constable, we stepped down and used the key from Mrs. Landry in order to let ourselves in.

"Right." Seaton clapped his hands together and looked about the vestibule. "Let's start at the beginning. I know we took a look around yesterday, but it was rather too quick to be thorough. Let's go over the house with a fine-tooth comb, see if there wasn't some other way for the murderer to get in and out. I find it hard to believe he sauntered through the front door."

"Hear, hear," I agreed. "Right or left?"

"Right," Seaton said decisively and led the way into the house.

I promptly relocked both doors so as to recreate the scene. My magical sight allowed me to see the wards quite fine, but it didn't allow me to see all the nuances. I donned a pair of magical spectacles in order to see things in a magnified way. I kept a wand balanced in the palm of my hand, searching for any other means of entrance.

The wards distracted me, making it a touch difficult to concentrate on the task at hand. The efficiency with which they'd been set up was so effortlessly perfect I found them enchanting. What a shame their creator met his end in such a manner, his life and brilliance cut uselessly short. I would have very much liked to sit and converse with him for an afternoon. It saddened me I'd never get the opportunity.

Shaking my head, I forced myself to focus. The front dining room windows were picture windows, not something that could be opened. I bypassed them and went into the kitchen. A single door led into a larder. The space was narrow, barely adequate to cook in. My partner would have a choice few things to say about the dimensions.

The kitchen window was the type to open, but so narrow I couldn't imagine anything larger than a child getting through. I tried it, just in case, only to find it stuck with humidity and warped over time. It barely receded two inches before screeching to a halt.

Of course, this experiment made the wards chime in warning, a heavy gong sound that was impossible to ignore or mistake.

"What was that?" Seaton called, alarm making his voice a touch shrill.

"Just me, sorry!" I called back to him. "I was testing the kitchen window!"

"Oh. Carry on."

Well, that at least proved the wards were in perfect working order. Even after the man's death, they operated as they should. I forced the window back in place, locking it again, and the wards settled into their happy thrum.

A slight frown tugging at my face, I went through the side kitchen door and into the hallway, but of course nothing led back there. A row of cabinets faced me, meant for storage, and showed no signs of being disturbed. The tallest of the bunch held the broom and mop and little else. I made note of it only because, aside from the stairs, there was nothing else for me to search.

I went back to the window, as any point of entry would make this easier. I started with garden variety spells meant to sneak through or disarm an active ward. They either slid right off, like water on a duck's back, or were repelled. I went through six before I cautiously put a shield up around me and tried a seventh. Just as well I had, too. The recoil of the spell hitting my shield knocked me back a foot and slammed my lower back into a knob. Wincing, I straightened and glared at the wards. Still working perfectly.

The wards fluctuated for a brief second, more like a reverberation from a strike, and I sensed more than heard Seaton also testing the wards. His magical strength could break them, I had no doubt. He was a powerhouse of magical ability, after all. But that wasn't the point of our exercise—we knew they could be broken. But could they be suborned and still outwardly seem to function?

Seaton bit off a curse that would make even a stevedore blush, and I winced. Perhaps it was time for me to intervene. This case had him hot under the collar as it was, and if I didn't stop him now, he'd lose his patience and really would masticate the wards.

Joining Seaton in the front, I found him pacing the length of the windows in the front foyer. They, too, were picture windows and completely impossible to open without force and broken panes. I wasn't sure why he was so fixated on them. "Seaton?"

He turned for just a moment, brows needled together, then gestured toward the windows. "If this magician was powerful enough to kill a retired royal mage, do you think he'd have been able to break a window and spell it back together?"

"Naturally. But we'd see some trace of the spell. I'm not detecting anything of that nature."

Seaton's shoulders slumped a mite. "I'm reaching, I know. This just doesn't make any sense to me. The wards are perfectly active. I see a few cleaning spells—there was some ash overturned here, I think—a heating spell, and a wind spell. All perfectly innocuous and reasonable for a mage's house. He'd use piddly spells like these on a near daily basis. Nothing points to the murderer."

"I feel your frustration and unfortunately empathize."

He snorted in dark amusement. "You say unfortunately because you'd rather be smug and have answers."

"Quite right."

"Cheeky." He flashed me a quick grin before sighing again, melancholy overtaking him. "I do not like this, Davenforth, I'll be frank with you. I came here for answers, and yet all we've done is confirm the same conclusion we reached last night. The wards have not been breached. However the murderer killed him, he didn't do it by magic. A gun seems more likely, but seeking spells didn't find one. I'd say one wasn't used, aside from..."

"Aside from the bullet wound."

"Yes." Seaton turned back toward the study, shoulders coming back up. "Let's look for that, shall we? Maybe we can find some answers."

That sounded quite the right track to me. I'd prefer to search for answers rather than beat my head against a blank wall.

I stopped where the chair still sat in the middle of the room and leveled my wand toward the wall. "Right. Seaton, you and Burtchell were about the same height, were you not?"

"Give or take two inches."

"Close enough for this exercise. Sit in the other chair, if you please. Let's see if we can't pinpoint something."

He obediently sat, although with a grimace, as sitting in a dead man's chair must feel strange indeed. I made this quick for his sake, using my wand to cast out a light in a small, steady stream towards the center of his forehead, miming the trajectory. "Right you are. Up, and follow it. Any trace of a bullet?"

"Not at first sight." Seaton moved the chair to the side for a moment, getting behind it.

The study was elegantly wallpapered in a light, silvery print on two of the walls, but the other two were covered in bookshelves. Including the area behind the chair. Seaton shuffled a few books back and forth, then let out a victorious, "Ah-ha! Good show, Davenforth. Looks like the bullet got stuck in the book. Oh, I say, that's odd."

"Seaton, I never like it when you say that word." I nixed the spell and went to stand at his shoulder, peering curiously. I saw quite quickly what he meant. The bullet was intact, its casing in place. It was a little squashed and misshapen, its nose flat, but that was only to be expected. It had gone through a human skull and partway through a book—of course it would be. But why was the casing still on it? This utterly baffled me. How in the devil did one fire a bullet and not remove its casing in the process? Even a misfire wouldn't do such a thing!

Proving his mind moved along similar lines, Seaton's dark eyes caught mine in utter bemusement. "Can one fire a bullet while keeping the casing?"

"I wouldn't have thought so. Certainly nothing in my experience suggests that's possible. Here, let me see it for a moment." I accepted the bullet from him and turned it over and over, my confusion mounting with every observation. "It was definitely used. I see a trace of blood here, on the back end, and its shape has been warped. It's definitely the right bullet. Seaton, when you did the spell, what was your search term?"

"Gun or other weapon," he answered slowly. "I suppose the bullet would slip through the loophole of the spell. Although technically, it's what killed him."

"Spells can be stupidly literal," I commiserated. Half my attention remained on the bullet, and I held it up towards the light of the window. "But see here, how the sides are clean? There's no real striation."

Seaton stared at me with a blank expression. "Striation?"

"Ah. This might not be in your experience. Do allow me to explain. When a bullet is used, the rifling inside the barrel will leave grooves along the sides of the bullet. Small, barely noticeable unless you're looking for them, but striations nonetheless. It's somewhat intentional, as the rifling is part of the reason why a bullet flies true. It's also part and process of a bullet being fired. It'd be quite impossible to leave these off."

"What if someone knew this, though? Removed the rifling from inside a barrel?"

"To what purpose? Very few know you can match a bullet with its gun—"

Blinking at me in a confounded manner, Seaton demanded, "You can?!"

"Something Jamie taught me," I admitted off-handedly. "If you can find the right gun, you can fire a bullet and match the grooves up. It's like a fingerprint, she claims. Impossible to miss."

Seaton growled out an oath. "We have *got* to persuade her to sit and record everything she knows about the criminal process."

"I say the same on a regular basis. I'll be happy to help you strongarm her."

He extended a hand, and we shook on it, as gentlemen do on an agreement.

"Anyway"—I turned back to the matter at hand—"this bullet was quite likely not fired from a normal pistol. Only a very ancient gun would not have a rifled barrel, and if such a gun was used, this bullet wouldn't have fit. It's too modern. And quite frankly, even from such a short distance, I can't imagine a bullet fired from an unrifled barrel would fly so true. That was the whole reason why they started rifling the barrels to begin with."

Seaton rubbed both hands over his face. "So we're looking for a strange murder weapon, on top of it all."

"Looks that way, old fellow." I frowned down at the bullet, lips pursed. "I do wish whoever had done it had used magic. I can think of a few spells off hand that would explain a bullet being in this state."

"I can likely think of a few as well, and I'm not an expert in murder like you are." Seaton looked about the room with growing agitation. "I don't like this, Davenforth. I don't like it at all. Someone was powerful enough to slip through a royal mage's wards, and yet doesn't use magic to kill him, but something else instead. Something so unorthodox that a magical examiner with years of experience can't even hazard a guess. At this rate, the murderer will get away with it just because we're not clever enough to figure out his methods."

I scoffed at this possibility. "Perhaps we're not clever enough, but I can assure you, my colleagues are better at thinking outside the box than we are. McSparrin has surprised me with an astute guess more than once, and that doesn't even take into account Jamie's mad logic. Don't write this off as hopeless just yet."

He did perk up a bit at that. "Perhaps you're right."

This was far unlike Seaton's devil-may-care attitude and I put a hand on his shoulder, looking up at him in concern. "Seaton. This is hitting close to home, isn't it?"

He looked away from me, towards the blank wall, and if it helped him to focus somewhere other than my eyes, that was fine. "It is. I'm not sure why. Partially because I knew the man, and liked him. Burtchell was an amazing man, a good friend to me, even though he had reason to resent me taking his position. Still, he showed me nothing but support and kindness. He didn't deserve an ending such as this. It also unnerves me; anyone as powerful and experienced as he was should have been safe within the walls of his own home. It's perturbing that he wasn't."

"I quite see your point." I wished I had magical words of solace to offer him but I came up empty. "The only thing we can do is solve how it was done, and create preventions against it."

Seaton inhaled deeply, then let it out slowly, and he looked more himself as he repeated the gesture once more. "Thank you, Davenforth. I became a little lost in this, I think. It's harder to process when it hits too close to home."

"Quite understandable. Well, we've found the bullet. Let's see if we can't find that magical research."

"Yes, where *is* that." Seaton turned in place and glared around him as if the very walls held secrets. "We've been through this house twice and I've not seen any hint of it. Is it small enough to be locked in some drawer?"

"I suppose we need to search more carefully and find out." I, too, was puzzled by the location. Most magical research occupies a full room, if not more. "You don't suppose there's a safe lurking behind one of these pictures, do you?"

"Only one way to find out. But first, what do we do with the bullet?"

"I've got a containment bag for it." As I turned to

collect my bag from the vestibule, I called over my shoulder, "Don't touch it with your bare hands or Jamie will skin you!"

There was a weighty pause from behind me. "But we already did."

Sodding deities. We had, hadn't we? I looked at the bullet in my hand and winced. Well, that was not going to go over well. I readied a mental apology as I placed the bullet into the bag and then locked it into my black bag. Nothing to be done for it now.

Seaton and I divided up the study and searched every nook and cranny. We assumed that to be the most logical place to start. Burtchell had spent the most time in this room, according to his housekeeper. Two of his desk drawers were locked, and they proved difficult in the extreme, shut down as they were by locking spells. I went through my arsenal of anti-locking spells to absolutely no avail and ended up scowling at the stubborn lock.

My colleague snickered at my struggles. "Some thief you would make."

"Like any thief would have the gonads to try and rob a royal mage, retired or not," I sassed back. Gesturing toward the drawer, I challenged, "You try."

He sauntered over and hit it with a spell, only to have that frizzle to nothing with barely a spark to show the effort. "Well, well, well, I see why you're struggling. He's used an Octagon lock. Clever man, weren't you, Burtchell? Hmm."

"Tell me we won't be forced to break the desk apart to get in."

"No, I think I can do it. It will just take more than a second."

I gave him space to work in, resuming his search on the other side of the room. The curtains hid nothing, the two landscapes in the room hid nothing, and I was about to take the bookshelves apart when

I noticed that the baseboard near the corner was ever so slightly detached from the wall. A wall safe? Or floor safe? Kneeling down, I poked and prodded at the area and finally saw the slightly indented space near the corner, perfectly sized for a man's thumb. I pushed down on it firmly and the floorboard popped up with a mechanical snick. "Ha!"

"Ooooh, floor safe?" Seaton's head came up like a dog with a new scent. "Is it under magical protections?"

"A few, two basic spells to be precise. I think he assumed the main protection was the wards of the house." This lack of protection didn't make sense otherwise. Unless, of course, the safe was empty.

These basic protections I knew how to clear and did so without true effort or fanfare. The safe was built into the floor, not just settled into a cavity, and it was the perfect size for a stab-bound ledger and not much more. When I opened the door, I saw precisely one ledger, bound in grey, and carefully levered it out. There were no markings on the cover, nothing to give a hint of the inside.

Flipping it open, I initially blinked down at it in confusion. I couldn't for the life of me understand what I was looking at. And yet, something about it was familiar...

"Seaton," I asked with slow deliberation, "by any chance was Burtchell involved with the study of Belladonna's work?"

"Indeed he was. Why? Oh bollocks, is that what you have in your hand?"

"I don't know." I levered up onto my feet, using the wall to assist me, so he could take a look. "But these inserted pages are in her handwriting. I've looked at it too much to mistake it for anyone else's."

Seaton stopped fiddling with the desk lock and reached out both hands. I put the ledger into them and watched as he flipped it about and stared at it hard. "You're right. That's Belladonna's handwriting. He's organized it and bound it together—we both know she wasn't sane or organized enough to do this—but it's her work. I'd consulted with him about it through correspondence. He was an expert in transportation magic. He was the perfect person to look this over."

We shared a speaking look. This information was definitely worth killing over. I wasn't sure why the killer hadn't searched for it—or maybe he had, and had done it so discreetly we saw no sign of it. Or perhaps he'd not had the chance. There was a lot of foot traffic in and out of the house that morning.

"I don't know what to do with this," Seaton admitted frankly. "It seems dangerous to leave the ledger here."

"I absolutely do not want it lying about in a house with wards that have already been defeated once. We'll abscond with it discreetly. Let's clear all signs of our search and set a trap in place. If someone does poke their nose where they shouldn't, we'll know."

Seaton nodded in agreement. "I'll get into these drawers, just in case he divided the information into different places."

"He likely did. The safe was barely large enough to hold this ledger." I eyed the desk with narrowed focus. "How long do you expect that to take?"

My friend let out a weary sigh that could have lasted him ten years. "That is the question, isn't it?"

And how long did it tak

Too long.

Far too long. Destroying the desk would have been faster.

Next time I'm doing so. Evidence or no evidence.

Report 06: The (un)Helpful

Very appropriately named chapter

why thank you

Penny ticked things off on her fingers as we walked along the main road. "We need to sort out who all had keys to the house, figure out who his early morning visitor was, and his schedule from the day before. Cor, but those last two will be a doozy to figure out, won't they?"

I grimaced agreement. "Unfortunately. What I wouldn't give for social media. But, the upside to this is that we're in a relatively small town. It shouldn't be too hard to figure out. It'll just take some legwork. Now, first question, who's the locksmith in this joint?"

Snapping her fingers, Penny agreed, "He'd know how many sets of keys are to that house. He would have made them. That's a good question. The constable will know, wouldn't he?"

"I'd assume so, but let's not walk all the way to the station just to ask a question." The day was already hot, and if not for the cool breeze coming in from the ocean, I'd be sweltering in my clothes. I didn't know why it was drummed into this society's heads that one had to be wearing a jacket in order to be 'properly' attired for public, but when I figured out whose brainchild that was, I'd wring their neck for it. Normally I'd just ditch the coat, roll up my sleeves, and be done with it. But unfortunately, on a job, I had to adhere to dress codes.

I could only imagine how Penny felt in her thick cotton uniform. It was a dark color, too, absorbing the heat. She wasn't sweating—yet—but I made plans to find a shaded and cool place for lunch.

At least trees lined the sidewalks and awnings framed the doors, giving us patches of shade to walk through. The area around here didn't have much in the way of trees, and the ones here were obviously planted by the townspeople. I appreciated their efforts. People eyed us in curiosity as we passed them, the ladies all in their skirts and parasols, the gentlemen in their light linen suits. It looked and felt like I'd dropped into a Jane Austen novel. Even after being on this planet barely a year, the sight was jarring to me at random moments.

"It seems a nice enough place," Penny remarked casually. Then she dropped her tone to complain, "Although I do wish they'd stop looking at us like we've sprouted a second head."

"Tell me about it. Two police officers, both females, always gets a double-take though. Not to mention Clint." I glanced down at my purple familiar, who trotted faithfully at heel like any well-trained dog. He glanced up at me, all wide-eyed innocence. Not that I'd accused him of anything, but with that look, it made me think he'd done *something*. I just hadn't asked him the right question yet. I did not trust that look.

Penny didn't notice our exchange, still complaining. "You'd think people would get used to it, what with the queen outright encouraging women to become officers."

"People don't change that quickly."

"There's truth." She eyed me sideways. "Were you surprised when Queen Regina came to you?"

I lifted a shoulder in a shrug. "Yes and no. Initially, yes. I don't really see her that often, and that she'd come in person down to the station alarmed me. That's not a woman who moves about at whim. But after she told me what was going on, I wasn't surprised. The Kingsmen aren't really experienced with murder. As crazy as this case is, it's still a murder investigation. I applaud her for the logical thinking: when you want a job done right, go to the experts."

"Us, in this case. Must be flattering, to have that much trust from her."

"It really is. I mean, she doesn't really know me that well, not as a detective." My mind went back to those early days, when I'd been taken to the palace to meet the queen. She'd been warm and friendly, full of questions. It had helped, to sit there and talk with her. I'd gotten a better sense of what I'd stumbled into. And knowing who my new monarch was eased my concerns.

"How's she, um, taking our updates?"

I recalled last night's conversation and made a face. "Mixed. She's happy we're more aware of the situation now, the nuances of the case, but she's not happy it's going to be difficult to solve. She's half-convinced it took a very powerful magician to murder a retired royal mage."

Penny obviously heard the doubt in my voice. "You don't agree?"

"No. I mean, think about it, if the wards had been tampered with, wouldn't the boys have said so yesterday?"

"But they're checking them now."

"They're checking them now because it's driving them up the wall. They don't know how the murderer got in or out, and they want an answer to that question. I mean, we do too. It'll help us solve the case. But really, if there was something wrong with the wards, they'd have been all over that like a fly on jam yesterday. And if it was a powerful magician who did it, why use a bullet to kill him?" I amended that to, "If it was a bullet. Weber's preliminary report didn't seem to point that direction. That straight trajectory is weird for a bullet's path. Still, if a magical spell had killed Burtchell, the boys would have seen that too. Makes me think the murderer used a more conventional weapon."

Penny let out a soft *huh*, a puff of air. "You're right. That doesn't seem to point to a magician. But then how did the person overpower Burtchell?"

"And that's the sticking point to my theory. How indeed." It did puzzle me, more than a bit, but I really had no idea. I'd seen what both Henri and Sherard were capable of on multiple occasions. Burtchell had been just as powerful as Sherard, according to everyone who knew him. I couldn't imagine someone overpowering Sherard. The only thing that made sense was that someone got the drop on him.

I spied a newspaper boy sitting on a collapsible chair, a stool next to him loaded with papers. A sign at his feet claimed the price for the morning paper and the early edition. If anyone knew the town like the back of their hand, the delivery people did.

I beelined toward him, pulling free a coin from my pocket. "Hey."

He looked up. The automatic smile on his face faltered as it landed on us. We did look an unlikely trio, I admit. His long nose twitched on his werefox face, and for some reason that made him even cuter. "Paper, miss?"

"Detective," I corrected him with a smile. What was he, eight? Ten? It was hard to judge ages with the weres, but his size and demeanor placed him young. "Detective Edwards. I wonder if you can help me with something? I'm looking for the locksmith in town."

Turning on his chair, he pointed further along the street. "Go down another block, take the first right, then go up three doors. Big sign near the door that reads McConnell's. Can't miss it."

I tossed him the coin, which he caught handily. "Thanks. Say, you wouldn't happen to deliver the paper in town, would you?"

"Sure do, miss. Uh, Detective." He wet his lips, his bushy tail flicking like an excited metronome. "You here to investigate the Burtchell murder? Constables said another set of detectives came in for that."

"Yeah, that's us," I confirmed easily. The reporters hadn't descended yet, likely because they didn't know who to talk to. I gave that another couple of hours, tops. Telling the kid anything meant his bosses would figure it out faster, but that was inevitable. "You can tell your boss if he comes to the Brighton Hotel and asks very nicely, I'll give him an interview. But if he shows up snapping pictures and being a nuisance, he won't get a peep out of me."

The kid actually saluted me. Sloppily. "I'll tell 'im, Detective."

"Good. I was going to ask, if you deliver, did you deliver the paper to RM Burtchell yesterday morning?"

"Didn't need to, miss. He caught me while I was doing my route, took the paper from me then."

Penny whipped out her small black book from a pocket. "What time was this?"

The kid scratched at his ear, thinking hard. "I'd just started, was only three houses in. So about five."

Five in the morning? "And where was he coming from, do you know?"

"Not sure, Detective. Somewhere further up in the hills. I was on Woodward Drive," he added helpfully. "And he passed me coming down it, so further up the road."

I was not above knocking on every door until I found the right house, so made mental note of that. "And he didn't mention why he'd been up all night?"

"Said he'd been playing cards and lost the time. I think he was going straight home from there."

"How far was he from his own house?" Penny inquired, still diligently taking notes.

"Mmm." Thinking about it, the werefox offered, "Maybe fifteen minutes? It'd be ten for me, but he wasn't so spry. I was surprised to see him walking, but he did walk the roads sometimes. Said it was good for his heart."

He'd retired after a mild heart attack. I wasn't surprised to hear he'd taken to walking for exercise. I wished I could get Henri to do the same. His eating habits were beyond unhealthy, and the man treated 'exercise' as a dirty word. He would develop diabetes or heart problems at the rate he was going. I shook my head slightly and focused. "You didn't see anyone else out, did you?"

"No, ma'am. Not until a good hour later. Milkman and postman both passed me as I headed to the paper company."

Not surprising, not at that birds' hour of the morning. "For the record, can I have your name? I might have further questions for you."

"Sure. I'm Best. Richie Best."

I winked at him and gave him another coin. Mostly because he was cute. "Thank you, Mr. Best. You've been very helpful."

"Anytime, Detective."

We walked on, following his directions.

Penny cleared her throat and asked tentatively, "You and Ellie Warner are working on increasing the speed of cars, you said. Isn't that dangerous?"

So she hadn't been completely comfortable on the ride here. I'd wondered, as she hadn't said much. Sherard was daredevil enough to enjoy it, and Henri was fun to torment, so I wasn't worried about them. "At the moment, your tires and suspension really aren't up to the task of a more powerful engine. We'll need to upgrade those things to make it feasible. But trust me, Penny, a car can safely go much faster. Cars on my world routinely go seventy miles an hour and sometimes above that without issue."

Her jaw dropped. "Seventy?! But a woman's uterus falls out of her body if she goes over thirty!"

I stopped dead in my tracks, neck creaking as my head slowly turned to look at her. She genuinely looked and sounded sincere, as if she weren't trying to pull my leg. "Penny. My dear friend. Where in the wide green world did you hear *that* bit of stupidity?"

Doubt clouded her expression, teeth digging into her bottom lip for a moment. "It doesn't? Or are the people on your world stronger?"

"Not noticeably, no," I denied wryly. Belladonna's changes on my body made me superhuman on this world. "Trust me, a woman's body can go through the same stresses and speed a man's can. We might not be as naturally strong as most men, but we're not weak. Not breakable. The next person who says such a stupid thing to you, laugh in their face. You've already gone fifty miles an hour and nothing happened, right?"

Penny's mouth opened, then slowly closed. "And we

were at that speed for several minutes. True, I didn't think of it that way. Actually, I'm not sure why I believed it to begin with. Dr. Sanderson said it."

"Really. Sanderson said it and you didn't automatically doubt the source?"

"He'd said it before I realized what a right twat he was," she defended herself. Then she shrugged, blue eyes sparkling with humor. "But now I can tell him how wrong he was, since we both did it just fine. Ha! That'll be good."

"Do me a favor: say it loudly and within my hearing. I want to watch the show."

She nodded immediately. "It's a promise. Are you, um, driving on the way back? Whenever we do manage to leave for home."

"Of course. I wouldn't miss tormenting Henri again for the world."

Why do you insist on scaring me?

You only have yourself to blame.

You have the best reactions.

Report 07: Strange Clues

McConnell's was exactly where Richie said it was. I did appreciate it when someone gave me good directions. Clint hopped off my shoulder to go chase a mouse he saw darting between the buildings and I left him to it. We stepped into the small shop, heard the chime of the bell over the door, and paused a few feet inside to get our bearings. The store wasn't all that crowded. A long counter wrapped like an L around the square-shaped room, and all manner of locks hung from the pegged walls on display. I saw precisely three safes on display to the far right, but otherwise the floorspace was clear. It smelled of beeswax and lemon, too, indicating someone had cleaned recently. This was a shop run by someone organized.

Which gave me hope that I'd get an answer. I called out in greeting, "Hello? Mr. McConnell?"

The infamous McConnell stepped out. I expected an older gentleman but instead found a fresh-faced young woman with inky black hair and an upturned nose. She wore a sensible dress of grey with a worn apron tied around her waist that hung oddly from the weight of various tools. She greeted us with a smile. "Ms. McConnell, actually. Ladies, what can I do for you?"

I pulled my suitcoat to the side to display the badge at my waist. "I'm Detective Jamie Edwards. This is Officer Penny McSparrin. We need to ask a few questions about one of your clients."

"Of course." She looked avidly curious but not alarmed as she gestured us closer to the counter. "What do you need to know?"

"Was RM Burtchell one of your customers?"

Understanding dawned over her face. "Oh yes. Everyone

in town is. The nearest locksmith aside from us is a two-hour drive."

Perfect. "Can you confirm for me how many sets of keys he had made for his house?"

"I certainly can. One moment." She stepped into the backroom for barely a minute before she came back, a file in hand, which she laid down on the counter so we could all see it. "It looks like we only have three orders from him. He had locks especially made for the house when he first bought it, several years ago. Not all locks are compatible with warding spells, you know."

No, actually, that was news to me. But then, I had a very faint grasp of everything magic could do. Partnering with Henri was teaching me the plethora of spells available, but I didn't always grasp magic's limitations. "And he gave you the exact specifications, I take it?"

"Oh yes. We wouldn't have been able to design them ourselves. That order took six weeks, it looks like. And then we created a set of keys for him." She flipped to the next page. "He ordered another set a week later for his house-keeper. Then about six months ago, he ordered a third set. Those were delivered to his solicitor. I believe they were meant to be held by the firm in case of his death. Part of his will, you know."

I understood that to be standard practice from anyone who didn't have relatives, or someone who had a designated estate executor that required access after the owner died. A solicitor kept the keys to the estate until it could be dissolved and dealt with. Hearing this meant RM Burtchell likely didn't have any close family, but I still needed to get in touch with his solicitor. It was on my growing list of things to do. But if that's the case, then I could account for all three sets of keys. "Do you mind telling me which firm has his keys?"

"Booker and Merritt," she supplied. "It's on Main and Cherry Avenue."

Penny made a note in her book before asking, "And there's absolutely no one else who had a set of keys?"

"No, not that we're aware of." Cautiously, she inquired, "Is there some issue?"

I might as well tell her. The papers would splash the news any day now, and she might have a hint of how the murderer got in and out. "When RM Burtchell was found in his home, the wards were up, his keys in his house, and both doors locked."

Her jaw dropped. "I'd heard he'd been murdered at home, but not that last part! I'm sorry, I can't help you. I only know of the three people who possessed keys."

It had been something of a long shot. I gave her a professional smile, struggling to not grimace. "Yes, well, thank you."

Penny surprised me by asking, "The keys. If the locks were specially made, were the keys that way also?"

"Yes. A magical element in them raised and lowered the wards." She snapped her fingers. "I should have thought of that. Wait here. I can get you the designs for the locks and the key, if that would help?"

I thought the boys would cry tears of joy to have *something* to go off of. "If you would."

She immediately turned and bustled back into her file room.

Giving Penny a nod, I praised, "Good thinking. I'm still wrapping my head around magic."

Her cheeks flushed a bit under the praise. "Two heads and all that."

"Yup."

The clerk came back out with an envelope, which she handed to me. "Here are the designs. I hope it helps catch whoever did this. RM Burtchell was a nice man. He did a lot for this town."

I'd heard the sentiment several times now, and it only made his death sadder. I really saw no motive for killing this man, but someone clearly had one. "We'll do our best. Thank you for the assistance."

We left again, and Penny asked me as we stepped onto

the sidewalk, "Where to next? Solicitor?"

"Solicitor," I agreed. "Might as well, since we know where he is. Then let's stop by the newspaper office."

She gave me an odd look. "You hate reporters."

"Not denying that. But I'd rather meet them on their own turf than be ambushed by them. And besides, I might have an idea of how they can be helpful."

We took a break around noon and retreated to the hotel. Partially because I needed shade from the heat of the day, partially because I knew their food was good, but mostly because we hoped the magical duo would have returned already. We'd missed the reporters at the newspaper company entirely—they were all apparently out on a story—and I wasn't sorry about that one iota. Still, it seemed a good point to stop and compare notes with each other before we started duplicating work.

Unfortunately, my timing was rotten.

The prophesied reporters were out chasing a story alright. Right here. They clustered around the front porch, near the side entrance. I had the feeling someone had moved them over there, away from the main door, and I could hear Sherard's confident voice rolling out as we approached. Press conference already in progress, eh? I'd not been forced to do one of those before, on either world, but I didn't hold out much hope I'd be able to skip this one. I was the lead on this investigation, and it wasn't fair to leave Sherard holding the bag.

Sighing heavily, I leaned in toward Penny's side and muttered, "Slip in through the back. I'll help Sherard deal with them."

She gave me a look that distinctly said *better you than me* before skedaddling. Traitor. I hefted Clint onto my shoulder to keep him from being squashed. He perched there like a pirate's parrot, looking about curiously.

The reporters stood about three deep, eight or nine wide. I saw the press bands pinned around their sleeves and recognized most of the major newspaper companies, including Sheffield's. I didn't recognize a single face in the crowd and was glad for that. The reporters in Kingston were vultures. Someone spotted my approach and let up a cry, and they were all quick to turn.

"Shinigami Detective—"

"Miss Edwards, would you care to—"

"Why did the queen call you—"

I ignored the lot and went straight to Sherard. He wasn't standing on anything to make himself taller, nor were chairs at hand. This was very impromptu and it showed. More than a few bulbs flashed as people snapped my picture and I sighed, resigned to the inevitable boost in rumors. These people, seriously. Sherard caught my eye and gave me a sympathetic grimace, then gave way and took a step back, giving me a sliver of room to stand in.

Yeah, no. We're not doing this. "Everyone back up! Give me some space to breathe. I will give you a statement and answer a few questions."

They jostled each other, eager for news, and gave me a whole foot and a half. I wanted more like a mile, but...oh well. I'd take what I could get. "Alright, I'm not sure what all my colleague has told you. I am lead investigator on this case. At this point, we don't know much. We have the basics of the case and we're still putting together a timeline and possible suspects. What I can tell you is this: Royal Mage Joseph Burtchell was killed in his own home yesterday morning, approximately seven o'clock. There's no question of it being murder. There is no possibility of either accidental homicide or suicide. It appears he did not see the murderer coming. At this point we do not have a firm opinion if the murderer was magical or not. I'm afraid there's not much else I can tell you."

The reporter directly in front of me was the first to get a question in. "Detective, is it true he was killed while his wards were up?"

Crap, I'd just known that fact would make the rounds quickly. A man that famous, a town this small, it was inevitable. Just as well I'd already resigned myself to that. "His wards were up when we found him, at least. We're still trying to figure out what happened."

"Detective," I couldn't see the speaker through all the other heads, but the voice was female, "Is there a reason why the queen called you and not the Kingsmen?"

"This is by no means a reflection on the Kingsmen's ability," I responded firmly. "It's more a matter of experience. Queen Regina has every faith in the Kingsmen when dealing with international and magical issues. But the Kingsmen are not accustomed to investigating murders. She wanted an expert for this case, to get to the bottom of it quickly. RM Seaton is with us as a representative of the Kingsmen, and he's aiding with this investigation."

"Detective, is there a reason you brought your own people here instead of relying on the local police?"

"They don't really have the experts here we need. There's not usually murders in Sheffield—lucky town!" I tried to joke and flashed them a smile. "It's why I brought my own coroner with me. The young officer with me, Penny McSparrin, is someone I'm training to be a detective. This case is perfect to give her experience. Doctor Davenforth is my partner, as most of you already know, so of course he came with me. It's quite a show for me to bring so many people, but it was more a matter of logistics and experience than anything. The local police have bent over backwards trying to help us solve this case. They've been entirely professional and amenable to me taking over, which I appreciate beyond words. I really need to get back to investigating that murder, so I'll allow one more question."

"Detective, do you know the motive?"

"Not at this time. But we're still pulling evidence together. I have faith we'll figure this out." I pointed a stern finger at them. "Now, off with all of you. I've work to do and I can't focus if you're following me about all the time. I'll issue another statement when I've got something to actually report."

It took more effort than that to get them to leave, of course. A few of the more tenacious reporters kept shouting questions at me, and I had to boot two of them physically off the porch. Constable Parmenter arrived on scene mid-process and helped us clear the rest of them away. Bless the man. By the time we were done, I was beyond famished and beelined for the dining room. Clint hopped down and went ahead of me, already leaping into an empty chair and curling up into it.

I reached the table to find Henri and Penny already close to finishing lunch. Henri pointed to the seat next to him. A covered bowl sat in place with enticing aromas of clam chowder rising from it. I dropped into the chair without ceremony and lifted the cover off with a sigh of pleasure. "You wonderful man. I could kiss you."

Color high on his cheeks, he gave a sage nod. "I reckoned you'd be half-famished. How did it go?"

"We got them to go away," Sherard answered, already tucking into his own bowl of chowder. "That's all that really matters."

"Hear, hear." I savored the first spoonful. So creamy. So delightful. Would they give me the recipe if I asked very nicely? "How did the search go?"

Henri took up answering the question as Sherard had his mouth full. "We did find his magical research. Seaton and I beat our heads against it for a bit, mostly out of curiosity, but we hardly needed to."

Sherard swallowed so he could pitch in, "Burtchell was an expert in transportation magic of all sorts. The story we've heard of him saving those ships? He did it by portal magic. He literally portaled three ships to the safety of the docks. That's how powerful and gifted he was with it. It's insane what that man could do. With him retired, he was the perfect person to handle the research."

With effort, I swallowed my mouthful, as I really wanted to ask the question I hadn't dared when talking with Sherard the other night. The boys were usually closed-mouthed about anything Belladonna related, probably in an effort to not dig at old wounds, and this candid conversation was rare on their parts. I wanted to capitalize on it. "Was he making any headway on figuring it out?"

"That's what we were trying to discern," Henri answered.

Sherard kept talking. "As far as we can tell, he had unraveled part of her notes. It's definitely a laborious task. Her handwriting is barely legible and her notes jump about. Still, he'd made progress. I'd like to read through the rest of it before we pass it back to the right hands."

I had to ask the obvious question. "Did it get him killed?"

"We're not sure," Henri answered with a shrug and a splay of his free hand. "Perhaps? It's highly valuable information, to be sure. But the research wasn't complete. Wasn't even close to it. And we saw no signs anyone had looked for it to begin with. They hadn't even used a seeking spell. Either they never got the chance, or it wasn't their objective to begin with."

"And we don't know enough to guess which it is at this point." Penny sighed deeply. "Lovely."

I shared her frustration. I also felt my appetite return and I squeezed Henri's hand in thanks before letting go. He gave me a soft, sweet smile before retracting his hand. "Any word from Weber?"

"We stopped in to see him earlier. He said the autopsy was taking longer than expected," Henri answered. "Although he didn't mention why. But I don't expect word from him until tomorrow."

"Really? I wonder why his plan changed. Did you discover anything else? Figure out the wards?"

Reminded, Sherard groaned and theatrically slumped on the table. Clint actually felt bad enough for him that he curled up on Sherard's shoulders, settling down and purring in comfort. It couldn't be comfortable to have an eleven-pound cat on your neck, but Sherard just patted him.

"That bad," Penny drawled. "Nothing hinky, magically speaking?"

"No, nothing out of the ordinary at all," Henri denied with a sigh. "Wards were fully functional—I tested that—all the windows either don't open or were still locked. The spells in the house were typical, something a magician uses on a regular basis. We did have one good stroke of fortune. If you choose to call it that. We found the bullet."

I clapped my hands together, tensing with anticipation. "So a bullet DID kill him. Where was it?"

"Directly behind the chair. It got lodged into one of the books, barely creasing the page. I was surprised it stopped there."

Shaking my head, I told him, "I've seen books stop a bullet before. All the layers of paper have amazing stopping force. But you should be happy about this; it means a conventional weapon was used. We have a lead."

Henri and Sherard exchanged a look loaded with meaning.

"We're not going to like this, are we?" Penny guessed wryly.

"I already submitted it to Weber for safekeeping, otherwise I'd show you," Henri apologized to us. "I thought it might help with his autopsy. But in short, no, the bullet is not helpful. The casing is still on it, to start with."

I blinked, because that was quite strange. "Maybe a misfire?"

"A misfire that went in a straight line?" Henri challenged, eyebrow arching.

"That...is a good point. Okay, so the casing was still intact. Anything else?"

"There's no striation on it."

I could feel my brain ground to a halt. "Excuse me? That's not possible. If it's fired from a gun, there's going to be marks."

Henri gave me a nod, expression deadpan. "You now understand why we are less than enthused."

It was Penny's turn to flop back in her chair like an over-dramatic actor. "Great. Because it's not enough we have a locked room mystery, but we needed a complicated and unusual murder weapon as well. What can even do that? Is there a spell?"

"A number of them, but we didn't see a trace of any spell like that." Sherard was still talking to the table top. Clint gave him a soothing pat on the side of the neck. "Just wind, heating spells, some minor cleaning spells. Normal things every magician uses on a consistent basis."

"Well, this is just getting better and better." I could feel a headache brewing. Figuring this out would require a lot of out-of-the-box thinking. My temples gave a painful twinge. "In better news, we have a more complete timeline for Burtchell's last morning. Paperboy saw him walk home at about five in the morning."

Henri looked intrigued. "Up that early or out all night?"

"Out all night. He was playing cards, the paperboy said. Somewhere further up the street. We have the approximate address. I'll knock on some doors after lunch, see if I can't figure out where and with who. We also found from the locksmith that the locks and keys were specially made to work with Burtchell's wards."

Penny's head flopped back upright so she could participate in the conversation again. "We have the designs for both, if you want to take a look."

Even Sherard sounded heartened by this. (Hard to see his face with a cat still on his neck.) "Sounds excellent. We'll do so after lunch. Anything else?"

"Stopped by the solicitor's—he had a key to the house as well, as part of the will—and while we didn't catch him, his paralegal promised to get us a copy of the will so we know how the estate is being broken up. Maybe inheritance money plays into this. I'd dearly love to lay my hands on a motive." I wouldn't hold my breath on it, though. Burtchell didn't live lavishly. The things he spent his money on were card games and race horses. His house was nice, and he had a housekeeper, but his lifestyle wasn't really over the top.

"I rather doubt we'll find a murderous relative," Henri denied thoughtfully. "I understand Burtchell to be an orphan. It made the news at the time, when he first was promoted as royal mage, that he did so entirely on his own merits."

"Never married or had children, either," Sherard confirmed, sinking back onto the table. "I'm not sure how much luck you'll have with this avenue."

"Boys. Don't burst my bubble. It's a nice bubble."

They just snorted and let it be.

I could see the waiters bringing plates of dessert our direction, so I reached over and snagged Clint, pulling him off. Sherard finally straightened, looking only slightly heartened at the sight of sugar heading toward us.

We'd eat, pray for a breakthrough, and go hunt down a potential witness. We had that list of associates from the hotel manager to get through. That would definitely eat up an afternoon, even if nothing panned out. Hopefully, either he/she or Weber would be able to give us an answer about *something*. Right now we had far too many questions and not nearly enough answers.

I don't like this mystery anymore. I no longer want to be Sherlock Holmes.

Who?

Ah, him. Wait, if you were Sherlock Holmes, who was Watson?

Henri, of course.

No, really, who in magic are you talking about?

Report 08: Magical Theory

As much as I'd like to sleep, I found it impossible to do so. The ladies had already stated their intentions to retire for the evening, but I stayed in the conference room with Seaton to pore over Belladonna's messy, difficult, hen-scratched notes. Why? Even I wasn't sure. The allure of the unknown?

Seaton had Burtchell's notes in front of him, I had Belladonna's in front of me, and we sat side by side, close enough our shoulders were in danger of overlapping. It was the only sensible way to handle matters. I had no desire to redo Burtchell's work, and his insights into Belladonna's portal crafting were absolutely riveting. I'd not seen magical theory like this since university. The last thing to break my brain in this manner was Jamie's attempt to explain hashtags to me.

"Am I reading this right?" I demanded of the man at my side. "Did Burtchell actually figure out how she powered the spell?"

"He did." Seaton let loose an incredulous oath that would have gotten him arrested in certain parts of the world. "Clever, clever man. How he dug that out of her notes is beyond me, but he's got two different reference points for it. Just that information alone is powerful."

I nodded in instant agreement. It was that. "No sign she put down source points or anything like that?"

"No, none. Have you seen any hint in her notes?"

"I've seen a few scribbles that could be it, but it's just as possible it isn't."

Seaton grimaced understanding. "Yes, one can break his own sanity trying to put reason behind everything she wrote down. Mark it, just in case. It might make sense later."

That was a sensible suggestion and I did so. We still hoped to find Jamie's path of origin. It was something of a moot point if Belladonna had written it down or not—at least in Jamie's case. Even if we could figure out how to send her back, we wouldn't. Her core was so unstable the trip alone would likely kill her. Even if she survived it, she'd be dead in a month. Magic—our type of magic—didn't exist on Earth. Without constant stabilization spells, she'd be dead shortly. Still, I wanted to find a way Jamie could at least send word back to her family that she was well. I knew it ate at her, that she'd left loved ones behind who assumed her dead.

Up until this point, I hadn't thought we could manage it. But knowing how the spells were powered, that was a game changer. It was an interesting quandary for me. As a magician, I wanted to know how Belladonna pulled it off. As Jamie's friend, I didn't. I didn't want to know and then have to face her and tell her she couldn't use it.

Seaton sighed in mixed regret and frustration. We resumed reading.

The door latch clicked and my head came up to see who had entered. Jamie strode through. Her hair was loose, and she wore the baggy shirt and pants she often wore to bed. Not that I knew what she normally wore to bed—well, I did, but that's because I'd been with her while she was convalescing. It's not like I had any other reason to...

I'm going to stop now.

"Henri, Sherard, why are you two still up?" She stepped lightly toward us, her feet bare and soundless on the carpet. Clearly she'd either been in bed or ready for it.

"We wanted to go over Burtchell's research," Seaton explained with no more than a glance at her.

"Seaton's called for a courier to come and fetch it tomorrow," I pitched in. "Tonight is our only chance to look at it."

"Ah. I did come down here to ask that very question, actually. The hotel manager said we could put it in the safe tonight."

Seaton gave a noncommittal hum. "We might do that."

Jamie came around behind me, her hands landing on my shoulders. I wasn't at all sure what she was going to do until her thumbs dug lightly into the upper trapezius muscles, right at the base of the neck, and I let out a low gasp of pain.

"Dude, you are *tight*." She continued to rub pressure around the shoulders. Her hands were knowing, sure, as if she'd done this countless times before.

I let my head drop, hovering between that border of pleasure and pain. It did feel good to have that tension released, although I was sure I'd feel sore tomorrow from it. I carried all the tension in my neck and shoulders.

"How much had he figured out?" she asked casually.

Seaton had to answer. I was too busy focusing on not drooling. "He figured out how Belladonna powered the spells. There're still no source points, or notes how she aimed the portal spells. I'm afraid that's going to remain a mystery. But for all her madness, this bit of craft is quite brilliant. It took someone of Burtchell's genius to unravel it. I haven't been this giddy about magical theory since university."

"Same," I croaked out and groaned as she hit a particularly difficult knot. "Oww."

"Are massage parlors a thing on this world? Because if they are, you need to go see one."

"They are, and we do." Seaton sighed and let the book fall onto the table with a soft thump. "After this case especially."

"Totally. So he figured out how she powered the portal spells? Isn't that the main thing that had you guys scratching your heads?"

"One of them, yes. It's actually quite ingenious on her part." Seaton, bless him, continued the explanation. "You're aware you can use an element as a source of power? Sunlight, water, wind, and so forth?"

"Sure, yeah, that's basic magical theory 101. Henri's told me that much."

"In this case, Belladonna used cosmic energy as an elemental source. Which is madness; that sort of energy can overpower and destroy a user if not harnessed correctly. Only the insane would attempt it. But of course, she was insane, and she managed. This much, at least, she was good about documenting. Likely because she had enough survival instincts to not rely on her memory. Her notes are jumbled, but Burtchell worked them out and put them in the correct order."

Jamie's hands stilled on my shoulders for a moment. "So...it's possible to recreate the portals? You always told me returning home wasn't doable."

"Still isn't," Seaton responded gently, apologetically. "We still have no source points, no idea which direction you came from. But we have pages of her notes we also haven't deciphered yet, so the answer might be in there somewhere. If we can make heads or tails of it."

"Sounds like you're not at square one, but you don't have that final solution, either." Jamie's tone was resigned but also a tad hopeful, her words taking an upward lilt.

"That's more or less the size of it. At least we've made progress. I didn't think Burtchell had managed any sort of breakthrough."

"There's that." She worked on my neck a minute longer before releasing me with a gentle pat on the shoulders. "Alright, I only came down to get that answer and pass along the manager's offer of the safe. Go to bed, guys, it's late. Night."

"Good night," we chorused as she left.

I did feel looser in the shoulders and neck, the strained twinges of a headache dissipating. Perhaps because of that, a thought I'd half-entertained earlier came back to me. "Seaton...are you done in?"

"Not really, my mind's still churning madly. Why?"

"How about we do a bit of our own magical ingenuity?"

He gave me a glance askance, one brow cocked in question. "I'm always game for that, as you well know. What?"

"Jamie asked me a question—well, it was more a complaint. But it sparked a thought. I'm not sure how viable it is. She reported to me that the postman heard a man visiting before the time of death, and that he was smoking with Burtchell."

"The postman's sure of that?"

"Werewolf," I explained succinctly.

Seaton's expression cleared instantly. "Ah. Yes, he'd know. Where are you going with this?"

"Wait, I'm getting there. Mrs. Landry claimed Burtchell only smoked cigars, that he never touched cigarettes, correct? We collected both from the study. Here's my thought. What if we take the cigarette and do a tracking spell from it, find the man smoking it?"

Seaton's head started to shake in denial, only for him to pause midway through. "But we can't track an owner of something, even something used?"

I lifted an illustrative finger. "*But* we can track blood from a person. We can identify parts of someone's body—like blood—as belonging to them. Why can't we combine both spells and use it to track the traces of saliva on the cigarette? There must be some."

He stared at me with wide eyes for a full ten

seconds. "That is quite possibly the most ingenious or the stupidest idea I've ever heard from you. But you know, I think it could work, provided we combine the spells in the right manner. You're sure it will work on dried saliva?"

"It works quite well on dried blood," I pointed out, glad to see he was on board with this idea. It was much more fun to work these sorts of magical challenges with a partner. And Seaton and I had proven to be a good team.

His imagination and intellect sparked. I could see it in his eyes as he swung about, heading for the chalkboard. "Let's try it. Wait, I don't want to do it with our evidence, what if we misstep on the first try?"

"That's quite a good thought," I allowed, thinking quickly. "And this might take us more than one try before getting it right. Let's see if the manager has a pack of cigarettes. We can try it with our saliva and get it nailed down properly before using it on our evidence."

"Go ask," he encouraged. He flipped the chalkboard about, scribbling out the nuances of the blood tracking spell. "I'll lay out the spells."

I dutifully went and fetched coffee while I was at it. This bore all the earmarks of turning into an all-nighter.

Morning light filtered in through the haze of cigarette smoke—not that I really noticed. My eyes were red and scratchy, either from the smoke or spending all night awake. Seaton was manic at this point, hair standing on end, in shirtsleeves and resembling a student right on the verge of a final test. Or perhaps a mad scientist. I'd cast aspersions at him if I wasn't positive I looked his twin.

But all of that was inconsequential because our hard work had paid off. And that made the sleepless night and our countless failures well worth it.

The door clicked open and Jamie strode through. Well, she started to. Her nose wrinkled up at the smell and she coughed. Waving a hand in front of her face, she demanded, "What are you two doing?"

Both Seaton and I were bent over the large table in the center of the room, at least a dozen butts in the ashtray, cigarette cartons strewn over the surface like a mother storm had hit. I beamed at her, possibly in a demented fashion. She looked both ready to bolt for safety and stalwart in her stance, clearly bracing herself for shenanigans.

Seaton bounded over to her like a puppy. He thrust an unsmoked cigarette at Jamie's face, nearly into her mouth. "Lick it!"

"You know, the last time I was naïve enough to fall for that line, I was six. I'd like to think I've learned better by now."

He waved it impatiently at her. "We're proving an experiment. Lick it."

Against her better judgement, Jamie gave it a good swipe of her tongue, eyeing him suspiciously as she did so.

Seaton carted the cigarette back to me proudly, like Clint would a mouse he'd just caught. I promptly waved a wand and cast a spell, the words lyrical. I reveled in a helping heap of smugness as the spell launched forward and a pale blue line shot from cigarette to Jamie in an unerring trajectory.

Of course she'd seen something like this before. I'd used a similar spell to track down a thief by using his blood. It didn't take a magician to be able to see the line, although not everyone could. It depended on how sensitive they were to magic. Jamie was just sensitive enough.

She stared at us incredulously, the facts tumbling through her head. The cigarette butt in Burtchell's study, the one Jamie had wanted DNA tested but couldn't. I could see her slot the pieces together visibly. "Correct me if I'm wrong, but there isn't a spell for what you just did."

"Not until, oh"—Seaton made a show of checking his pocket watch—"an hour and ten minutes ago."

Jamie promptly went to him, seized his face with both hands, and kissed him right on the forehead. He spluttered a laugh, then laughed harder as she turned on her heels, snagged me, and did the exact same to me. I blushed and cleared my throat, finding it difficult to meet her eyes.

"You're both freaking brilliant and I love you for it. Have you tried it on the butt from the study?"

"Not yet," I denied, fussing with the hem of my waistcoat and still blushing hotly. "We wanted to make sure we had it down before we attempted it. Just in case the spell went horribly wrong."

"Thank you for being sensible. Well, it's breakfast time now. Don't take this wrong, but you two need a bath and a change of clothes, at least. Let's stop, eat, compare notes, and then do your spell afterwards."

I immediately agreed with relief, "Yes, let's."

As proud as I was of my success, I did reek of smoke. And with the elation wearing off, I desperately wished for rest. Perhaps I could fit in a nap later on in the afternoon?

Seriously brilliant work, gentlemen.

Aw, you're making Henri blush!

And not you?

I own my genius.

Of course you do.

Report 09: Location, Location, Location

I felt somewhat more refreshed after a quick bath and a change of clothes. We met up after breakfast and sorted our agenda for the day. As it wasn't necessary for all of us to follow the potential lead of the cigarette, we divided duties once more. McSparrin went to check up on Weber, as he was far later in finishing the autopsy than expected. Seaton fell to examining the lock design of the house to see if he could find a way to lockpick it. Jamie and I used the lead from the cigarette.

For some reason, Jamie insisted this tracking required the use of the motorcar. Of course, with me casting the spell and maintaining it, I could hardly drive at the same time. Which defaulted to Jamie driving, and truly, I didn't think that wise. I eyed her with open dismay. "Surely we can walk?"

"In this heat? *You* want to walk somewhere?" Jamie riposted neatly, an impish grin on her face. She patted my arm consolingly. "I promise I won't go over fifteen, alright?"

"I'm holding you to that." With severe misgivings, I climbed into the passenger side of the vehicle.

She started the motor as I cast the spell. I had the cigarette butt in the palm of my hand, with a glove on to keep from contaminating it, my wand in the other. Our variation on the Blood Hunting spell meant we had cannibalized the basics of the spell and then incorporated it to detect water—saliva, in this case—instead of blood. A weird gestalt, to be sure. I still wasn't quite sure why it worked. That particular bit of genius was Seaton's brainchild more than mine, and I'd been so dizzy from lack of sleep I'd let him try just about everything. Including things neither of us should have tried.

I spoke the incantation carefully, it being very new to my tongue. "Water of the body, hear me. Hear the call of your source. Return to your origins. Show the path to the one who holds you." It worked just as expected, the line leading out further down the street, stretching out of sight. The traces of saliva lit up in wisps of blue and white, wrapping about the butt before flowing ahead, illustrating the path to follow. The line appeared as a steady blue stream, unlike its sister spell, which showed red.

Jamie put the car into drive and we were off, both of us keeping a keen eye on the thin blue line.

"It really is quite cool," Jamie complimented me. "You and Sherard should publish this. Do magicians publish papers?"

"Quite so. A limited circulation press issues a magazine on a quarterly basis. I've never contributed to it, although Seaton has on a few occasions." I was flushed with pride that she thought this spell so revolutionary it was worth sharing with my peers. "You think it that remarkable?"

"Not only that, but helpful. Think of how many cases you could have used this spell to find a suspect. And if it works with saliva, would it work with something else? Tears, or skin cells? Hair?"

My interest perked sharply at the implications. "I hadn't thought of it in that respect. We'd only just gotten it to work, after all. You think it would work on a, well, not-liquid part of a body?"

"It all belongs to a person's body, doesn't it? I think it would still gel." Her confidence was spoiled as she added, "I think. I don't know, I'm not a mage. You tell me."

"In theory, I allow it's quite feasible. We'll have to experiment after this case and see how it all is." I'd also like to test why the tracking spell worked on her. I would have thought that with all her immunity spells, one would have failed. I'd nearly stopped Seaton before he demanded she lick the cigarette, but I'd wanted to see the results. We still struggled to grasp exactly what spells were deemed as "harmful" by Belladonna's spellwork. This one apparently did not fall under that domain.

Jamie's mind continued on in a different vein. "I hope you have time to experiment properly after this. I just know this case is going to open a can of worms."

"I'm sorry?"

"Ah, right, that idiom doesn't translate well here. I mean it's going to open us up to potential trouble. You know how the kingsmen want me to join their ranks?"

I nodded. I'd heard that before. Several times, in fact. After seeing the way the kingsmen reacted to her, I was rather surprised she hadn't already done so.

"Well, I can just see this case opening up the debate all over again. If the queen has enough confidence in me to come to me directly, then why aren't I in the kingsmen?"

Oh dear. I did see her point. "By your tone, I assume you don't wish to go to them?"

"I might, eventually. It does hold some appeal. I have a lot of friends there. But I have to admit it doesn't feel like the right option to me right now. I really don't understand enough about this culture to be in that high of a position. And frankly, I'd miss working with you too much."

My heart warmed at this sentiment, one I shared completely. Although it also worried me that she might leave in the future. I'd not known what to do with a partner in the beginning of our acquaintance, but now having experienced it, I was loath to lose her. "I'd much prefer you stay."

She flashed me a smile. The sun caught her just

so, lighting up her eyes, turning her skin even more golden, and she looked picture-perfect in that moment. It distracted me utterly for a moment.

"Even if I do steal your chocolates?"

"Speaking of, you owe me a box. Don't think I don't know where that last one went."

"Now, Henri, maybe you ate it without remembering."

I scoffed at this and bent a glare on her, fighting to keep my mouth from twitching up and betraying my humor. "Ha! Is that really what you're going with?"

"Maybe, instead of just buying yourself a box, you should buy two. One for me, one for you." Her eyes were on the road, leaving her in profile, but I didn't have to see her face clearly to know she was laughing internally.

"I don't suppose the concept of just buying your own chocolates has occurred to you?"

"That sounds like a lot of work and not nearly as much fun."

Rolling my eyes, I prayed for patience. Until this game became dull, she wouldn't stop anytime soon.

The line we followed took a detour. It didn't follow roads, of course, more a course the crow would fly. It meant taking several different turns, attempting to keep it within line of sight, and sometimes backtracking when a particular street didn't go the way we predicted. If we'd been in Kingston, we'd not have needed to backtrack or guess nearly as much. I knew the streets well there, after all. Being on unfamiliar ground left me vaguely uncomfortable.

After twenty minutes of driving the streets, I found myself heartily glad we weren't walking this after all. Jamie was sedately staying within normal speeds too, keeping to her promise. I'd compliment her for the good suggestion if I didn't fear it would go to her head and make her speed up.

We wandered our way into the residential area

in the hills not far from where Burtchell's bungalow sat. Eventually, the line went through the front door of a house more seaside cottage than anything fancy. It looked very much like a vacation house, not large enough to comfortably hold more than six people. Even that might be more a stretch. The house was made of white planks that gave off a charming air. Carefully tended flower beds bracketed the doors and lined the paved pathway to the front door. I ended the spell at that point, as we more or less had our location. It alarmed people to see a magical line attached to them, and doing so with a magician attached sent them into a tizzy. Ending it now gave them a chance to gather themselves and I didn't have to deal with accusations and the like. If, by some chance, the line had alerted the murderer, and he took the chance to bolt? I could also renew the spell. But I'd rather play this cautiously at the start.

Jamie parked and shut the car off. We both exited the vehicle. Neither of us looked at each other or said a word but we were both anxious about this meeting. The timing was suspicious enough to incline us to believe that this person knew something about the murder, and it might give us the lead we desperately needed.

As we approached the house, I observed the nation's green-and-gold flag was at half-mast. A white ribbon of mourning hung over the doors and windows as well. Was this house grieving someone?

Deities take it, of course we'd stumble into a house of mourning. The tensions inside would be lethal. My shoulders hunched in grim anticipation.

Jamie took it all in with a glance but it didn't dismay her. She strode right to the door and knocked on it firmly.

The door was opened a moment later by a stalwart looking woman, long in the face and body, her bearing stiff with pride. White touched her temples, and the fine wrinkles around her unsmiling eyes leant an age to her person. I mentally placed her in the same generation as Burtchell. She was not, to my surprise, in mourning white.

"Hello," Jamie greeted in that professional manner of hers. "I'm Detective Edwards. This is my partner, Dr. Henri Davenforth. We have a few questions for someone in your household."

"Oh. Yes, you must mean Oscar. I told him to go to the constable, but the man's so distraught, you can barely get three words out of him at a time." She waved us inside with a fixed smile on her face, looking badly adhered on. "I'm Priscilla, Priscilla Villarreal. Come through, please."

Unlike Burtchell's house, this one had a more open floor plan, and I was immediately able to see through to the formal sitting room. I could hear the sound of water boiling and pots being shuffled about through a closed door I assumed to be the kitchen. Mrs. Villarreal led us through the sitting room and out the back, onto a covered patio that offered blissful shade and a cool sea breeze to keep the edge of the heat off. A stodgy man sat in one of the chairs, staring blankly out, oddly dressed in a warm cable sweater and thick pants and boots, as if chilled. Grief sometimes felt like shock to a person. Perhaps he experienced it as such.

I discreetly cast the spell again, double-checking we were indeed facing the right man. The line stopped at him and I silently cancelled the spell, pocketing my wand. One look at him, and I knew this wasn't our killer. This man was shaken to his core over Joseph Burtchell's death. The lines of grief in his face were so deep he seemed a hundred, although he couldn't have been more than sixty. He was ravaged by loss. Our murderer had killed Burtchell in cold blood face-to-face. It took a different type of emotion altogether to do that.

"Oscar," his wife said with some compassion, coming over to lay a hand on his shoulder, using physical touch to draw his attention to her. "Two policemen are here. They want to talk to you about Joseph."

Oscar Villarreal turned to regard us with puffy, red-rimmed eyes. "You are?"

Stepping in closer, Jamie offered a hand, which he took. They did not shake, however, with her holding it in a more sympathetic manner. "I'm Detective Edwards. Queen Regina appointed me and my partner, Dr. Davenforth, to investigate his death. May we ask you a few questions about him?"

He nodded faintly. Mrs. Villarreal settled onto the seat next to his, keeping an arm around him in a supportive manner. We took the two chairs facing the low settee, Jamie reclaiming her hand as she settled. I let her take lead on the interview, as he responded readily to her.

Jamie pulled out her ever-present little notebook, readying a pen. "May I ask your relationship with him?"

"We were dear friends, ever since he moved out here." Villarreal spoke in a rasp, his hands winding in and around a handkerchief in his lap. "He didn't know many people here. I bumped into him casually in town, as one does, and invited him to a card game. Didn't know he was such a sharp at the time. He was ever going about, helping people with things. Loved to use his magic, you know."

I did understand that perfectly. Magic liked to be used. It felt uncomfortable for a magician to go any real length of time without using it in some manner or another.

"Can you tell me about the last time you saw him?"

"Well. It was the morning he died, actually. We'd been playing cards up at Benny's—"

"Benjamin Walterson's," Mrs. Villarreal interjected

for our benefit.

Her husband barely noticed, still speaking. "—and it went into the early hours of the morning, as it often did. Us old people don't sleep much. He'd walked home after that, and I did the same, when I remembered he'd asked me for a favor. Seems his car was giving him some trouble, and he wanted help taking it to a garage. I stopped in at his house to see what time he wanted to deal with it. We smoked, talked about his winning at one of the races the day before, decided to celebrate it a bit...." He trailed off, fresh tears brimming in his eyes.

No wound hurts more than the possibility of happiness thwarted. That, I knew achingly well. It would haunt him for some time, not being able to share that small celebration. "You smoked the cigarettes, I take it?"

Mr. Villarreal blinked and turned to me as if just now properly seeing me. "What? Oh. Yes. He never did like them, said they were too small for a man's mouth. Preferred black cigars."

"What time did you leave?" Jamie asked gently.

"I don't know."

"He got home at nearly seven, and it takes him ten minutes to walk between our houses," Mrs. Villarreal filled in for him.

Mr. Villarreal nodded, as if agreeing.

"Did you see anyone on the way?"

He didn't just respond, he paused and truly thought about it for a moment. "The paperboy. The mailman. He'd dropped off the post while I was there. Joseph collected it as he showed me out."

"Mr. Villarreal this part is very important. Was there anyone else in the house, anyone at all, before you left?"

Mr. Villarreal shook his head immediately. "No, no one."

I'd expected the answer, and yet cursed it. Jamie's expression said she felt the same.

"And can you tell me if he locked the doors behind him?"

Mr. Villarreal stared at her, unblinking, for a long moment. He opened his mouth, then closed it, seeming to go back to that morning. "You know, I believe he did. The wards on his house, they always made this deep hum sound when they first kicked on. Like a queen bee, you know the sound? I heard that as I was leaving. It wasn't unusual. Joseph liked his wards up. Only way to do that, he said, was to lock the doors. That's just how it was designed."

I mentally went through every curse and foul swear word I could think of. I'd hoped he'd give us some sort of clue on another visitor. Of how the doors came to be locked with a dead man inside and no suspect. But of course this case wouldn't be so neatly solved.

"Do you know of anyone who was angry with him? Or had any issues with him?"

He immediately shook his head.

Jamie changed the question, softening it with a gentle tone. "I've heard he liked to gamble. Was he in any debt because of that?"

"No, Joseph was good with his finances. Careful managing the vice. We don't usually play for money, anyway. Play for peanuts. Most of us old folk up here aren't flush. Joseph was, but you never really knew it talking to him. He just liked to play."

I knew Jamie wouldn't leave it at that, and she didn't. "There wasn't anyone angry at him for winning? Accusing him of cheating, or anything like that?"

That brought a brief, watery smile to the man's face. "Often. But it was always teasing, never in earnest. People liked to say he had used the magic up his sleeve. He lost too often to make him a real card sharp, though."

"I see. I'm going to change topics, ask you about something else. The research he was doing, did he say anything about it?"

Mr. Villarreal stared at her hard, and I could see the figurative light flicker on. "Detective Edwards. The Shinigami Detective?"

Her smile turned rueful. "Yes, people like to call me that, for some reason."

"Oh. I'm sorry, I just realized who you were. Joseph was studying you, he said. How you got here. He didn't speak of it much, just that he'd been handed this glorious puzzle to try and solve."

"Did he mention this to anyone else?"

"Just those of us who were in and out of the house. Maybe a handful of people. Why do you ask?"

"Right now, I'm searching for a motive," Jamie admitted frankly. "Someone hated this man enough to kill him, but I can't see any motive for it."

"You think it was the research? Someone wanted it?"

"It'd be very strange if that's the case. We found it in his study. I'm just asking questions at this point, trying to get an overall picture. You can't think of anyone who was angry with him?"

"Well, some were over the sunken ships." Mrs. Villarreal patted her husband's hand. "Remember, Oscar? He got all those nasty letters for not saving all the ships." To us she explained, "There were five ships in danger that night, nearly two weeks ago. The storm was so brutal no one could get onto the sea to help them. Joseph was called in and he used his magic to transport three of the ships to the docks, saving them from being dashed against the rocks. The other two were too large, he said, he couldn't save them. He did get some of the crew and passengers off before they went down. But some people thought he should have done more and sent him all sorts of letters calling him out. It upset Joseph terribly."

I shared a glance with Jamie. That sounded like a potential suspect pool.

"Did anyone come to his house? Come up to him personally?"

"I—" Mrs. Villarreal paused and shared a frown with her husband. "No, no one did. I think he would have said if someone had."

"A few people actually sent apology letters afterwards," Mr. Villarreal tacked on. "Joseph went and recovered the bodies from the sea, you see, so people could bury loved ones. It healed some of the grief."

Alright, maybe it wasn't such a good potential suspect pool after all. I mentally groaned in frustration. If Burtchell's closest friend couldn't think of anything, that didn't leave us many places to turn.

"Thank you, Mr. Villarreal. I'm going to leave my card with you. If at any point, you remember something else, you can find us at the Brighton Hotel. We're staying there while we investigate. I'm so sorry for your loss."

He dredged up a watery smile. "Thank you, Detective. I do feel a little better, knowing the queen sent you both herself. I trust you'll find the person who did this."

"As to that, sir, we're doing our level best. We don't take any death lightly." She gave his hand another squeeze before standing.

I stood with her, following her out, Mrs. Villarreal showing us the way. She paused at the doorway and eyed us both fearfully. "You don't think my husband did it?"

"At this point, it seems highly unlikely," Jamie answered. "Your husband's testimony matches up quite neatly with every other witnesses'. I'm not inclined to suspect him. Mrs. Villarreal, I couldn't press him on this point, but did RM Burtchell have any enemies?"

"Not here," she answered, a relieved hand pressed over her heart. "He was a hero here. He might have had old enemies in Kingston, from when he was still a royal mage, but he didn't mention them if he did. He was quite at peace here. And Oscar and Joseph loved each other so, like lost brothers who'd found each other. It was heartrending when we heard the news. Thank you for not suspecting him, that would have destroyed him utterly—that anyone could think he'd harm Joseph."

Jamie gave a sad smile. "I know that. I've seen it before. Please, encourage him to reach out if he thinks of anything else, alright?"

"Yes, of course."

"Can you tell me where Benjamin Walterson lives?"

"Oh yes." She rattled it off from memory, which I jotted down. Another round of goodbyes and we were able to leave the house.

We turned for the car. As I walked at her side, I leaned in to murmur, "Not the news we were hoping for."

Jamie groused, "It feels like we're back to square one. Hopefully Weber has something. Otherwise, we're going to be spinning in circles."

"What do you want to do now?"

"I think it's time to get a second opinion about the gambling. Let's go talk to Benjamin Walterson, shall we?"

Report 10: #Witnesses

Benjamin Walterson had to be the most unremarkable person I'd ever made acquaintance with. He was a weredog—not a common race, to be sure—and he was *still* unremarkable. Not an ebony pelt, or a rich ermine, or anything pleasing to the eye. Just a regular, dusky tan that looked frazzled around the edges. His whiskers kept twitching on his face, as if he were one second from a sneeze that never seemed to arrive. Shirt untucked in the back, missing a vest button in the middle, and collar popped up on one side, he was the epitome of a slovenly gentleman.

He stood on his doorstep and blinked at us quite owlishly from behind his spectacles and then jerked them off, pointing them at Jamie. "I say! You're the detective in charge of Joseph Burtchell's murder, aren't you?"

"I am, sir," Jamie responded levelly. She held out a hand, which he shook without really looking at it. "Detective Edwards. This is my partner, Doctor Davenforth."

"Oh, pleasure, pleasure. I'm Benjamin Walterson. Come in. Sorry for the state of the house, the missus has been in a right state ever since she heard about Joseph. Won't leave her sunny spot in the garden for all the world. Says it's the only place she feels any comfort. It disturbed her deeply, it did, that ours was the last card game he played. Might not be able to host another game for a long while. Come on through, sit here—oh, no, best not, let's sit at the table, it's clear there, and—"

I let the man prattle on without even trying to get a word in edgewise. The house was indeed in a state. Evidence of a party lay on every possible surface, and not much effort had been made in cleaning it up afterwards. I catalogued discarded playing cards on various tables, half-filled glasses, plates of peanut shells and other sundry finger foods, and the air smelled stale and sour with the leftover remains of food and alcohol. My nose twitched and I suddenly understood why Walterson's kept doing the same. I did feel on the verge of a sneeze.

The main room was so thoroughly taken up we had to skirt sideways to gain the dining room. Someone had the windows wide open there, and it appeared Walterson had claimed the space as his own, attested by a discarded paper, a pad and pen, and a half-drunk cup of coffee.

"Can I get you a cup?" he offered as we took the sturdy wooden chairs on the other side of the table.

"No, thank you, Mr. Walterson," I demurred. "You know why we've come to speak with you, I take it?"

"I've got a jolly good idea, yes. Sorry I didn't come in sooner. Truth is, after the card party, I left. I took the early morning train into Crammer's Port, slept on the way there. My daughter's at university there, you see." A wide, proud smile crossed his face. As well it should. It was difficult for women to go to university, and if she were attending Crammer's, then she was very bright indeed. Crammers was a well-known medical school.

Jamie pulled out her notebook. "You went to visit?"

"She had a spot of trouble," Walterson explained, getting more settled in his chair, and further rucking up his shirt against the back of it in the process. "Some dastard knocked the books right out of her hands— she did say it was accidental—and then refused to pay for their replacement. She needed the books for class today, so I went up and bought her a new set. I was gone till...well, I did stay long enough to take her out for an early lunch. Came back in the afternoon."

"And that's when you heard?"

"Impossible not to. Word was all over the place. I was heartbroken at the news, we all were. It's such a bloody terrible business." He sighed deeply, a rough growl echoing deep in his throat in a manner only a canine could produce.

"Can you tell me who was at the party that night?" Jamie continued calmly.

"Oh, yes. I've actually been writing it all down. I think I've got everyone. I'd ask my wife, but"—he grimaced here with an apologetic look—"she's too distraught, you know. Can't get a word out without bawling."

I took the list from him and scanned it. Twenty-six people. A respectable enough gathering, especially for a house of this size. "And did anyone have harsh words with RM Burtchell that night?"

"No, no. We were all in high spirits, in fact. Burtchell was on something of a losing streak, could barely keep a hand in. It was odd for him, but he wasn't upset about it. Just a string of bad luck. He kept laughing and changing games, seeing if that would help. Nothing did, but it didn't stop him from playing." Walterson's face fell, his pointed, upright ears going down and flat. "He did love to play."

Jamie pressed him, although she kept her tone level. "Did he mention any trouble with gambling debts? Or someone who took issue with him winning?"

Walterson's head came back up and his whiskers twitched again as he thought. "No. No, can't say he did. But he wasn't the type to blab his business about, either. Oscar might know. Have you spoken with Oscar Villarreal?"

I nodded. "We just came from there. He couldn't

think of anyone."

"Well, there you have it. If Oscar couldn't think of anyone, then there isn't anyone to be had."

Jamie didn't quite roll her eyes, but I was sure she did so internally. "Clearly someone did have issue with RM Burtchell, Mr. Walterson. They killed him, after all."

"Oh." Walterson's ears went down again. "That is a good point. Yes, that's a very good point. Oh dear. Well, what I can tell you is, no one was in a murderous frame of mind at my house, at least. We all left in good spirits, if tired after a full night of fun. I saw Joseph out myself, and he walked home alone. I went into town and caught the train shortly afterward."

And that didn't help us whatsoever. Although the list of people at least gave us something to look at.

"Thank you, Mr. Walterson." Jamie stood, signaling the interview was at a close. "Here's my card. We're staying at the Brighton Hotel while investigating everything. Please contact me there if you think of anything else."

"Yes, yes, I'll be sure to. Thank you, Detective. Doctor."

Walterson politely showed us out, and I was glad to escape into the clean, fresh sea air. I was tempted to take the wheel so Jamie couldn't drive us back into town, but in truth I was sleep-deprived to the point of exhaustion. It was better for her to drive us back. She caught my false start for the driver's side and gave me a knowing look as she slipped into the seat.

As she started up the engine, I inquired, "I suppose we start in on that potential suspect list?"

Jamie looked at it with a resigned sigh. "Yes, although I don't hold out much hopes for it. This case smacks of rage, but also cold calculation. It took someone very clever to get past all those wards, and it wasn't done in a spur of the moment. If this was a case of someone accusing Burtchell cheating at cards, I'd think they do something more on the spot, rather than finding a way to sneak into his house."

"I rather agree with you. But we don't have any other leads to follow, not really."

She stared at me hard, head canted. I knew that expression well. She was weighing the pros and cons of something. "You think the magical research he was doing is a dead end?"

"We did find it all in his house," I reminded her.

"Granted, but it could be the murderer just didn't have time to search for it, either. I think we should ask the queen."

I blinked at her and felt more than a little alarm at this idea. "You want to ask her? Surely there are other people to ask!"

"Sure there are," she agreed casually, already taking out her pad. "But Henri, that woman is desperate not only for updates, but to be able to help. She's delegated this investigation to us because she's a: smart enough to realize she wouldn't know how to investigate, and b: responsible enough to know she can't. But it doesn't mean she's not invested, that she doesn't want to help. Trust me, keeping a woman in the loop is always a smart decision. You might not get any real help from her, but you'll be considerate of her feelings, and that leads to happy things later."

Considering my own history with my mother, sister, and now my partner...she made a fair point.

"And the woman's been blowing up my pad with requests for an update," Jamie tacked on while making a face. "If I don't talk to her soon, she's going to send the Kingsmen after me."

"Ah. Well, I can play scribe for you?"

"Hmm? Naw, it's fine, I'll just call her." I felt a little horrified when she casually pressed the phone spell button and commanded, "Call Queen Regina."

It barely took two seconds for the call to connect and the queen's tinny voice responded eagerly, "*Jamie! Tell me you've good news.*"

"I wish I could. I actually called with a question for you. You might be able to help us."

The change was audible in the queen's voice. She went from eager to tautly alert. "*Yes, of course, please ask.*"

"We found some of Belladonna's paperwork in Burtchell's study, along with his own notes. I understand he was researching the portal spells?"

"*Yes, so he was. I asked him to take it on, as really there is—was—no better expert. He was very happy to have something to mentally cut his teeth on, or so he said. I'd get random reports from him that he was making some headway, although I hadn't seen anything he'd done. Why do you ask?*"

"We're stuck on a motive for his murder." Jamie wrinkled her nose in distaste, not that the queen could see the gesture. "We're not sure why anyone wanted to kill him. Everyone in Sheffield apparently loved him, and despite all the card games he liked to play, he rarely did it for money. It doesn't look like gambling led him into a tight spot. I thought, maybe someone was after the research?"

"*But you found it intact in his study, did you not?*"

"Well, I don't know if we did. There was no sign of forced entry, or that anyone used seeking spells to find it, but it's feasible he had part of Belladonna's work on his desk when the killer came in. The man was reading a letter at the time of his death, after all. Who said he didn't step away from his work for a moment to look through his mail? How much of Belladonna's work was given to him?"

"*I'm not entirely clear on that. But I know who to ask to find out. You sent what you found at his house back to Kingston?*"

"Sherard did this morning, by special courier."

"He likely sent it to Langley. She's in charge of Belladonna's work and cave, as you know. Langley will be able to tell if something is missing. I'll have her get in contact with you as soon as she has an answer."

"That would be very helpful, thank you. Ask her, too, if anyone's shown any unhealthy interest in that research, or if anyone made noises about it. Is Gibson still in charge of all that?"

"I believe so. I'll have him message you with anything he knows."

"I'd appreciate it. Be patient, Your Majesty. I know you're chomping at the bit to know who did this, but this is early days yet. We're still putting together a timeline. I at least know who all was in the house and how narrow of a window the killer had now."

"Oh? How long?"

"About ten or fifteen minutes, it looks like. A very narrow window. It suggests to me that whoever did this was watching Burtchell closely. They must have, to have taken such perfect advantage of that gap in his defenses. It's why I wonder if the magical research had something to do with it. He didn't apparently tell many people he had it, but he did tell a few. And a few is sometimes all it takes."

"Sadly true. Oh, is it that time already? Monkey balls. Jamie, I've got to go, I've a function to attend, but I'll contact both Langley and Gibson on the way. Keep me updated, I implore you."

"I promise I will. I'll speak with you later." The connection ended and Jamie sat back with a sigh. "That was more or less the answer I expected, but maybe we'll get lucky and either Langley or Gibson can point us in the right direction."

I gave her a flat look. "You realize if either of them had heard of potential trouble surrounding that research, they'd already have contacted you and said something?"

She screwed her mouth up in a strange looking pout. "What is it with you and bursting my bubble? I like my bubble."

"Don't hand me a line, woman, I know better."

Pointing imperiously forward, she commanded, "Let's just go. Cross-check Walterson's list with the one the hotel manager gave us to eliminate any duplicates. We'll still have quite a few to get through, and we still have to find all their addresses."

As Jamie started the motor up, I lodged in a final protest. "We're stopping midday for lunch."

"And dessert," she added firmly.

"Deities, yes." With multiple interviews to get through, we'd both need it.

Report 11: Magic Bullet

"The bullet killed him."

I regarded Weber with considerable exasperation. Jamie looked ready to skewer him with her eyes alone.

"Tell us something we don't know!" my partner exclaimed, throwing up both hands.

After twelve straight interviews today (all conducted at the witnesses' houses, which meant a great deal of driving about town), neither Jamie nor I were in a particularly patient mood. Twelve was better than twenty-six, but we had still done a great deal of legwork with little result to show for it, and the feeling grated. I certainly wasn't in the mood for Weber's cryptic remarks. I wanted answers, something I could sink my teeth into and give me the necessary momentum to solve this case.

We were in the conference room, basically awaiting Weber before getting dinner and calling it quits for the day. The hardest thing to learn when first becoming a detective was how to pace oneself. Too often, especially in high profile cases like this, the colossal pressure on the investigating team pushed them to work incredible hours. But unless the case demanded speed—such as kidnapping cases—it was unwise to work like that. For one, it burned out even the most dedicated workers. For another, it dulled the mind and senses. Many a case had been bungled or left unsolved because the investigating team was too tired to properly manage the clues right in front of them.

Jamie, fortunately, was seasoned enough she knew better than to fall into that potential trap. Although I might have to stop her from coshing Weber's head in.

Weber was clean of any blood or ichor, yet I could see the work he'd put in the past two days by the tired sloop in his shoulders. He sat slumped in the head chair of the table, his bag at his feet, ready to report to us and leave.

"I'm sorry for the delay. I had a hovering doctor at my elbow who slowed me down considerably. Sadly, there wasn't much else I discovered," he stated, voice rasping with fatigue. "I went over every part of the body three times, looking. The bullet oddly told me more than the body did. Good job for finding it. We'd be up a creek with no paddles otherwise."

In a very Jamie move, Seaton held a hand up to me. I played along and smacked mine against his, completing the "high-five," as she called it.

Weber seemed amused at this byplay, if that quirk of his mouth was anything to judge by. "Brace yourselves. I'm about to add to the strangeness."

McSparrin made a disgusted sound and glared at him. We all more or less imitated her. *More* strangeness was the last thing this case needed.

Undeterred, our coroner kept going. "The bullet was not fired from a gun. There's no trace of gunpowder residue around it. The blood splatter on the back is a perfect match to Burtchell's. It was definitely the bullet that killed him, I'll stake my reputation on it, but it was not fired from any sort of weapon."

That more or less confirmed what I already knew. I hadn't tested the bullet for gunpowder, but that was more because I didn't have the right equipment to test it. I'd requested Weber do it for that very reason. He'd come more prepared in terms of equipment than I had.

"Now, what is interesting to me is the trajectory angle. What I believe happened is this." Weber stood, then went to McSparrin and gestured for her to turn in the chair to face him. She promptly did, acting the part of the deceased. "I believe Burtchell was sitting, reading his mail. The killer came in with the bullet in his hand, like so," Weber held his hand at hip level, much like he was in the act of reaching into a coat pocket, "and somehow fired the bullet from there. It was in a perfectly straight line, only a little off-center from the epicenter of his forehead and angled slightly upwards. I believe Burtchell was looking into the eyes of his killer when he was shot."

"So," Jamie pointed to the two of them, reasoning out loud, "Burtchell perhaps wasn't expecting another visitor? Or this wasn't necessarily someone he knew? He was just sitting, reading his mail, and this guy walks in. He looks up, then bam! Lights out."

"Quite possibly. I can't say for sure. I can say there's no defensive wounds, no signs he struggled or was even properly aware of the danger. The doctor's report to me was that when they found Burtchell, both of his hands rested in his lap, one hand gripping the letter. I don't think he had time to react to his assailant."

"How did the murderer even get in, is my question." Seaton sounded one breath away from beating his head against the desk.

I shared the frustration, but mine was fixated on another point. How was the bullet fired if not from a gun? Was it magic, after all? I couldn't think of a single device that could fire a bullet without somehow leaving a mark on the casing. But if it were magic, that made less sense. None of the spells in that room had been in the least remarkable, all of them expected from a mage's house. Had the murderer somehow wiped his own magical footsteps, erased his presence altogether?

"Seaton, focus for a moment. Not on the entry point, but on the means of firing the bullet. Is it possible to erase magical energy from an area?"

Seaton stared with dark amusement, brows quirking. "You felt stupid for asking that, didn't you?"

"Yes, quite." I sighed morosely. "No need to rub it

in. I just can't think of how this was accomplished."

Weber seemed intrigued by our discourse and paused where he was, eyes bouncing between us. "Why is it impossible? To do what you're suggesting."

"Magical energy is much like…air. That might be the easiest way to explain this." I rubbed at my jaw, trying to put this in layman's terms. "It's quite impossible to block air completely from a space, correct? It's much the same with magical energy. It flows and is part of everything. You can't dismiss it, especially once used. It disintegrates on its own."

Jamie cleared her throat. "Actually, you can suck all air from a space. It's called a vacuum."

We all blinked at her.

Perhaps feeling a little put on the spot, she added, "Takes very specialized equipment to do it. And you definitely feel it."

Truly, the things she knew…. I waved a hand. "Perhaps not the best analogy to use, then. At any rate, what I'm suggesting is truly impossible. Fortunately for us investigators. A criminal using magic can never completely erase their tracks. Muddle, yes."

"This might be a case of muddling." Seaton crossed both arms over his chest and sank back in the chair. "I feel like we're missing the obvious."

"You might be," Jamie pointed out. "It's easy sometimes to lose your perspective and not see the forest for the trees. Let me play devil's advocate for a bit. Walk me through each spell you saw traces of in that room."

Seaton didn't feel inclined to play and waved me on. I'd learned to humor Jamie in situations like this. It might not bring about an immediate answer, but often it raised the right question that led us further along. We could use either at this moment. My mind felt foggy with fatigue, and at the moment I regretted every minute I had stayed awake to create a new spell instead of resting, like a sensible person, and tackling it the next morning. My focus was more on a nap even as I answered, "Very well. Cleaning spells."

"That one seems obvious enough. How old was it?"

"The night before, I would say. It was barely distinguishable."

"And the next?"

"Heating spell. It was centered around a cup, also from the night before."

"And the next?"

"Wind spell. Dead in the center of the room."

Jamie got a strange look on her face. "And you're not questioning this one because...?"

"It's quite often used to either clear the air of smoke or to cool a room. Considering the cigar and cigarette, it's natural for it to be used."

That strange look on her face didn't leave. "And it was used right afterwards?"

"Well, yes, or thereabouts. We arrived so late on scene I couldn't tell you precisely. The spell had disintegrated by that point."

Seaton pointed a finger at her. "I know that look. You don't agree with us."

"It's just, I know you have very valid reasons why the spell was used, but I don't see why it couldn't be the culprit. Couldn't a wind spell be used to fire a bullet?"

I opened my mouth to deny this claim, then paused when my brain clamored with possibilities. It left my jaw hanging as I sat there, possibilities whirling like a dust storm. My eyes met Seaton's and I could see the same realization dawn.

"She's right," he breathed.

"Of course she's right, she's always right. You'd think we'd be used to that by now." I kicked myself for not realizing it earlier. "Blood and magic, we're both benighted fools. Theoretically, Jamie, you're quite correct. I could see how a wind spell might be adapted to do that very thing. But let's not put our full stock on this just yet. I think this bears experimentation. If we can get it to work, and duplicate the state of the bullet now, then we can discuss it. And after I get a nap."

"Fair enough." She grinned at me. "Feel better now?"

"I think we all do. At least we have a possibility." I gave her a thankful smile. She was truly gifted at getting me unstuck when I was too mired in my own assumptions to see daylight. "We'll consider other means of how to fire a bullet from waist-height if this doesn't pan out. Weber, excellent work. Thanks for making the trip."

"I can't say it was my pleasure, I'd prefer not to work on cases like this, but at least I hope it helps get the poor man justice. Just a note, while his heart was somewhat damaged, he was doing alright. I think he'd have lived another ten years with decent health before declining."

So whoever killed him had robbed Burtchell of those years. That news sent a pang through my heart.

Weber collected his bag, readying to go. "Best of luck to all of you. Call me if you need me, but I hope you won't have another body on this case."

We all threw up a sign to ward off bad luck, although Jamie oddly enough rapped her knuckles against the table. I really did not understand her mannerisms sometimes. Shouldn't you toss bad luck over your shoulder?

As Weber left, I stood and stretched myself. "I say we stop here. We could all use a relaxing dinner and a chance to let our minds rest. Seaton, we can buy some cartridges and a board tomorrow, do our experiments somewhere along the beach."

"It'll be cooler there," he agreed. "As long as we can erect some shade to keep the sun out of our eyes."

"Sounds splendid."

Dinner was quite delightful, all told. I egged Jamie into telling the story of one of her more interesting cases she'd worked on Earth. It led to all of us relating a strange case we'd been on, and the conversation flowed freely. Clint, for some reason, took up residence in my lap during the course of dessert and stayed there, draped over my legs like a woman's castoff fur stole.

We all went our own ways after dinner, finding some peace for ourselves and unwinding. I took a brief stroll outside, enjoying the coolness of the evening, before eventually retreating to my own room. I found myself still too alert to think of retiring. A second wind, of sorts. It was a clear sign I'd been awake too long and my body's rhythm was thrown off. That, or the nap I'd had earlier was playing havoc with me. At any rate, instead of sleeping, I picked up one of the few journals I'd brought with me. It was quite interesting so far. Ellie Warner's medical breakthrough regarding distilled alcohol for cleaning was in there, and even though I knew how it worked, I still found the article riveting. Ms. Warner had a talent for keeping a reader's interest.

I settled into a chair near the open window, enjoying the sound of the sea crashing against the rocks below, reading by lamplight.

Some time had passed when a knock sounded at my door. "Henri?"

"Come in," I invited, already putting the journal aside. My eyes automatically found the small clock on my bedside table and I noted the hour with some surprise. It was well past anyone's bedtime. Why was Jamie here?

She entered with her usual confidence. For

some reason, she thought little of entering a man's bedchamber. I found I could not reciprocate the attitude. It still made me nervous to be in hers, despite the necessity of the action on several occasions. Her coat was missing, as was her vest, but she still retained the tie she'd worn earlier. It hung crookedly and from one hand, as she gingerly held it close to her chin.

"This stupid thing has gotten caught in my hair," she explained with a wince. "Can you untangle me?"

"Of course," I assured her, hastily standing and gesturing her into the chair. "Is it badly tangled?"

"Badly enough I can't seem to pull it free. I think a strand escaped my braid somehow and it's been slowly tangling in with the clasp all day. When I went to take the tie off, it yanked hard." She settled, one leg tucked under another, her back to me.

I'd assisted either my mother or my sister with similar problems in the past. I tilted my head to get a good look at the situation, hands gently tilting her braid upwards. "Ah. Yes, you're quite correct, a strand has gotten quite firmly tangled around the clasp."

"You can cut it free if you need to."

"Let's not be so hasty. I believe I can detangle you." The first rule of tangles was to start at the bottom and work your way up. I set about the task with gentle fingers, carefully pulling the lock of hair in and around the metal clasp.

"I'm glad you're still up. I expected to find you snoring."

"I'm punch drunk, as you'd put it. Too tired to sleep."

"Ah. Should have figured. I'm glad you are. Clint's cute, but useless for stuff like this."

The image of Clint trying to untangle her hair amused me and I chuckled. "Although I'd have paid to see him try. Is he happy, being here with you? He seems quite pleased."

"Oh, he's over the moon. It's unfortunately going to start an argument when we get back. Now he'll think he can go on every murder investigation."

"I don't see why he can't assist us on at least some of them."

I could see her surprise, and she almost faced me before she thought better of the action. I still had my fingers buried in her hair, after all. "You think?"

"He was quite helpful in scouting out the roof and crawlspace," I pointed out reasonably. "He knew what to look for and it saved us the trouble of sending a grown adult into uncomfortable places. I know you think of him as a companion, but he *was* created to be a magician's familiar, you know. He has the intellect to assist you."

"Well, yes, I know..." She trailed off, her expression thoughtful. "I suppose I didn't consider he's like a dog. I can train him to help me. He's just such a furball sometimes, I forget what he's capable of."

Clint would thank me for this later. "I'm sure if given a chance, he'll prove helpful in many ways."

"I'll talk it over with him. How goes it back there?"

"Almost free. Fortunately, it was more wrapped up than truly tangled." Her hair was silky and thick, but not so fine it liked to tangle in those insane knots. My sister was very envious of Jamie's hair. I'd heard more than one complaint about it. "There. You're free."

She pulled out the tie, freeing the braid altogether, and ran her fingers through it, shaking it loose with a sigh of relief. "Freedom. Thanks, Henri." She popped up and kissed my cheek, grinning into my startled face before bouncing out the door. "Night!"

I stood stock still, flabbergasted and reeling. Did this woman not understand how attractive she was? She flustered even *me*, and I was accustomed to spending time with her. I really must teach her that casually kissing men's cheeks like that was just not done. She'd seduce someone at the rate she was going.

I took myself quite firmly to bed, determined to sleep. Clearly, with my current mental state, I needed it.

I'm going to enjoy this.

What? No. Don't be absurd.

huh?

Nooooooooothing

Report 12: Target Practice

Seaton and I set up shop on the beachfront overlooking the water, with a large shaded umbrella off to the side. The area here was more gravel than sand, which suited our purposes. It prevented sand from sneaking its way into my shoes. We both discarded coats as well, rolling up our sleeves in concession to the heat. With no ladies present, we were thankfully at liberty to do so. Although I did rub a healthy amount of sun-shielding potion onto my skin before beginning. I still had winter skin, having spent most of this year within doors.

We had a board propped up, its back overlooking the sea. We felt it safer to fire over water than any other direction. Misfires would likely plop harmlessly into the water this way. Since we knew precisely what caliber of bullet to work with, we bought three cases of those, two thermoses of cold water, and several paper targets.

It felt better to be in my element, even if I were outside my lab. I preferred research and experiments like this, things with easily definable results. And Seaton was an excellent partner for such things. Really, it was the best of all worlds.

Assuming I didn't get as sunburned as a lobster.

We stood safely in the shade of the umbrella and each took up a bullet, only to pause and stare at it dubiously.

"I'm not entirely sure how to use a wind spell to shoot a bullet from my bare hand," Seaton finally admitted to me. "Would it work on the same principal as a firearm?"

Immediately, I shook my head in disagreement. "No, not possible. Do you know the mechanics of how a gun fires?"

"No, do enlighten me." He said this sincerely, curiosity brimming in his dark eyes. "I only know the principal of how to shoot and clean a gun."

It didn't surprise me. I assumed most people who didn't actively either use or manufacture guns wouldn't know the mechanics of it. Seaton, especially, had magic as his weapon. Why would he know how this worked? "To put it simply, when the trigger is pulled, it causes a firing pin to strike the primer—this section here, at the base of the bullet. When the primer ignites the gunpowder, the burning powder creates pressure inside the barrel. That pressure pushes the bullet down the barrel and out."

He stared at the bullet with understanding. "So striking the bullet itself does no good in this situation, as there's no chamber for it to build pressure in."

"Quite right. It leaves me at something of a loss, however. I wonder..." I stared at a sailing ship far off in the distance. "Windwhisperers often direct wind in controlled fashions to propel ships forward. I wonder how they do it?"

"They can't just haphazardly call on the wind, it'll capsize the boat." Seaton also stared hard at the sailing ship. "Perhaps by creating a small vortex at the base of the bullet, it will create the necessary force to propel it forward?"

"It's as good as anything to try. Do the honors."

Seaton spoke the spell, crafting it to hit the bullet and only the bullet, precisely. It was a pleasure watching him work. His expertise over magic was infinitely fine, like poetry in motion. I barely had a chance to see the spell in action, so quick was the movement. The bullet shot from his hand and landed on the edge of our target board. And by landed, I mean to say it took the corner clean off.

We stared at it in consternation.

"Bit too much force, there," I suggested mildly.

"And it didn't fly straight, either." Seaton frowned at the missing corner as if the bullet had gone that direction for the sole purpose of irritating him.

"Perhaps a touch of funneling around the base of the bullet?"

"As a control? Seems sound, in principle anyway. Try it."

I altered the same spell he had used, hoping to stabilize the bullet's path. The magic warmed my core as it activated, the wind chilling my bare palm as it caught the bullet up. In a flash, it was gone, shooting through the air with the same velocity as any gun could produce. It did not land on target center, but a clear hole hovered near the edge of the bullseye.

"Oh, I say, that did much better. Not nearly as destructive. That seemed the right amount of power, didn't it?" Seaton trotted over to take a closer look at the bullet hole in the board, humming in a pleased way.

"I wonder if varying the speed of the vortex will stabilize its flight path?"

We fell to experimenting, making minor adjustments here and there. In the course of an hour, we riddled the board with holes, so much so that we had to stop and change the target three times in order to mark our results. After a certain point, we stopped and sat in the shade, drinking heartily from our chilled thermoses.

Seaton stared at the board in between healthy gulps of water. "Davenforth, I think we're more or less on the right track. I know we're not hitting the center of the bullseye consistently, but I think that's general marksmanship on our parts. Neither of us are used to firing anything physical. And magic has its own guiding feature; it follows our intent on hitting the mark."

I nodded agreement. "We're truly out here just to prove the theory right or wrong. I think we've done that. What interests me, and I think you'll agree on this point, is that it takes very little in the way of magical power to use this spell. In fact, it worked better with limited power."

Seaton's expression turned hard and unhappy. "Yes, I'm quite of the same opinion. It looks less likely with every clue that a powerful magician killed my colleague."

"I'm rather grateful. I'd prefer not to have powerful, murderous magicians running about," I said dryly. "On the other hand, it does leave us with a rather wide suspect pool."

Snorting, he shrugged. "It's less helpful in that respect. Jamie often tells me you don't need to know motive in order to solve a crime. I can't help but think, though, if we knew the motive, we'd be able to find the murderer."

"You too, eh? I've entertained the same thought more than once." I took another sip, the water blissfully cool as it slid down my throat. One of the many advantages of being a magician was that your beverage was always at the correct temperature.

"Perhaps we should start by listing out every magician who would be able to use a wind spell? I know it's rather a long list, but Jamie will ask for one."

"That she will." I hesitated, considering our next move. I'd really rather not do it, but I could see the drain in Jamie every time she updated the queen. She never complained of it, but it taxed her, and this case was stressful enough. I'd like to offset that, if I could. "Perhaps we should take a moment and update Queen Regina? She'll be pleased to hear we've made some progress."

Seaton regarded me thoughtfully. "I thought we were leaving that thing up to Jamie?"

"Seaton, really, she definitely isn't the right person to report this."

"You sound all reasonable, but I know very well you have an ulterior motive."

I sometimes thought this man was friends with me solely for the enjoyment of poking at me. "Isn't there someone else you can tease? Friends, relatives, poisonous reptiles?"

He snickered but let me be, pulling the pad from his jacket pocket and dutifully updating Queen Regina. I glanced at the screen to keep track of the conversation and saw he'd looped Jamie in as well. Excellent. That way we didn't have to go over this with her again later. I did detest repeating myself. I leaned in at an angle so I could read over his shoulder.

Of course, Queen Regina asked the question we had no answer to: *Do you have any suspects at this point?*

None, I'm afraid, Seaton wrote back in his elegant cursive. *We have various facts and theories, but nothing substantial enough to point to either motive or a suspect.*

Absolutely nothing incriminating? she demanded again.

Jamie chose to join in with her own quick, blocky writing. *Patience. I'm still going through people who knew him.*

Seaton thankfully backed her. *Investigations take time. Not much we can do to speed the process along, I'm afraid.*

I see. I don't mean to rush you, but I want an answer to this.

That was royal-speak for Get It Done. I didn't need Seaton's commiserating glance at me to translate that.

Jamie: *We're doing our best. Bear with us a little longer.*

I will trust you. I must go, I have a meeting. Thank you for the update and hard work. Queen Regina left at that point.

Jamie surprised me by continuing the chat. *If you're done, come back. Need some help.*

On our way, Seaton wrote back. *I think we're done here.*

"Yes, quite," I agreed. "Let's pack quickly. I wouldn't mind some luncheon and to sit on something padded for a while."

As we made the trek back up the narrow stairs to the hotel, irritation flashed through me. One would think, with all the tourists they had through here, the steps leading down to the ocean would be better maintained. They were so cracked and crooked in spots, it was difficult to go down them, never mind up. I was winded and sweaty by the time we reached the hotel's terrace, and wished desperately I could take my coat off again. I hit myself with a wind spell to cool down, then Seaton too, for good measure. His wand was in use to levitate the umbrella and the two thermoses; he wasn't in any position to do additional spellwork.

"Bless you." He sent a quick smile in my direction. We temporarily separated there as he left to return the umbrella.

I continued on to the conference room, depositing the boxes of leftover cartridges, board and targets on a receiving table near the door with considerable relief. The board had dug into my hands on the way up, cutting off circulation in a quite uncomfortable manner. I flexed the digits to restore blood flow as I turned toward the two women. Perhaps I should have used a levitation spell as well, although I'd been afraid of banging the board into everything on the way in. Levitated objects were often like a dog's tail—they hit things they shouldn't. "Anything new?"

"Yes and no," Jamie answered with a nod toward McSparrin, who was settled at the table. Jamie herself was at the chalkboard we'd had installed for our use, carefully writing out a timeline. "Penny's been reading through Burtchell's correspondence, and it seems like it wasn't all sunshine and roses after all."

My ears perked up. Drawing a chair away from the table, I gratefully sank into it, my attention riveted on them. "Do tell. He had enemies?"

"I'm not sure if they were enemies, per se," McSparrin returned a touch doubtfully. "But more than a few people sent him letters or cards, saying what a shame it was he only saved the three ships. And why hadn't he picked one of the others to save instead? Seems quite a few sailors lost their lives on the two ships he didn't save."

I shook my head in disbelief. "I know Oscar Villarreal mentioned this but it still boggles my mind. The man saved *three ships* from sinking to the ocean floor and he gets castigated for not saving them all?"

"Most of these people are relatives of the ones lost." McSparrin waved one in particular to illustrate her point. "I think it was grief speaking more than anything. They were upset with him, but I'm not sure if they were upset enough to kill him. I've even found three letters that followed after the first, where the women who'd written to him apologized for saying anything."

"Hasty words said in a moment of anger. Or written, in this case." Jamie was still frowning at her chalkboard timeline. "I'm not inclined to think our murderer is in there, although we'll still need to check them out. A person who's willing to tell you off in a letter either doesn't have the balls to follow through in real life, or they find catharsis in sending the letter. Generally speaking. There's exceptions, of course."

"Hence why you want to interview these people." I knew her to be correct. I'd seen similar cases. "It gives us a possible suspect pool, if nothing else. I'm quite inclined to speak with them."

"Not like we have any other leads. I seriously doubt at this point our card-going suspects are going to have anything helpful to add. We still have ten left to clear, but so far everyone has solid alibis and no motives. Oh, and Gibson contacted me just now."

I could tell from the look on her face it wasn't helpful news. "Let me guess. He didn't know of anyone who wanted Belladonna's research?"

"Well, he does, but no one who knew Burtchell had it for study. Langley also reports that what we sent to her was all Burtchell had. Nothing's missing. So either the murder has nothing to do with his research, or the murderer just didn't get a chance to search for it before the housekeeper arrived."

Penny rolled her eyes doubtfully towards Jamie. "Which one are we going with?"

"Research as a possible motive. Because frankly, even though I don't think it's very plausible, I have no other possible motive. Until we find something more suspect, we'll continue to look at it."

"At least we know *how* he was murdered," Penny muttered in disgust. "Sort of."

"Yes, good job on the wind spell." As predicted, Jamie turned and queried hopefully, "And what kind of magician can use a wind spell?"

"Basically? Most of them. It's a rather basic spell." Her face immediately fell and I reached out, squeezing her hand gently. "Sorry. I did make a list for you to consult. In essence, anyone above a second level student could do this spell. Wind spells are basic enough they can all employ them, but the level of control it took to fire off a bullet in your bare hand? I would say second level, at least. Students, hedge wizards, windwhisperers, licensed mages, crafters, and even magical examiners could all be suspects."

"So, most of the magical practitioners in the country." Jamie threw up her hands. "I can see why you're not all that excited about this."

"If it helps any, I don't believe our killer is a very highly skilled magician. The amount of power to fire the bullet isn't much, and the more power we put to it, the more uncontrolled it became. I think we're also looking for someone who does something similar with wind spells on a consistent basis. Seaton and I both agree it would take practice to be able to hit a target reliably while utilizing such a spell."

"And out of those professions you just listed off, who would use a wind spell consistently?" Jamie was poised at the board, ready to take notes.

"Hedge wizards—they're called such because they are often used by farmers, miners, or even tanners to aid in their profession. They use elemental spells more often than not. Crafters, for similar reasons—they're focused on crafting different tools and spells for market. You've seen the bottled wind spells sailors sometimes buy, to aid them during the dead spots on the sea? Crafters create those."

Jamie not only took notes on the professions, but what they included. She started with my native language, then defaulted to hers in an effort to keep up, only throwing in the occasional native word. I sympathized with her frustration, but at the same time, I wished she wouldn't do that. She'd master Velars faster if she stopped defaulting to English. Perhaps I needed to spend more time helping her study the language.

Shaking the thought away, I finished, "Windwhisperers use it the most, by far. In fact, they use only three elemental spells, for the most part. They're utilized on the larger ships to keep them sailing."

"And which of these are most likely?"

"You're fishing," I accused her.

Seaton chose that moment to rejoin us, and he

asked, "Who's fishing for what?"

Turning my head, I explained to him, "She wants to know what profession is most likely to shoot air bullets."

Seaton shook his head at her. "You're fishing. You realize you can find an abundance of crafters, hedge wizards, and practicing mages out here? They gather most of their needed elemental material in places like this."

"And it'll be hard to even track down a windwhisperer on land. They're normally on a boat somewhere at sea," I added.

Jamie pulled a face, nose scrunching up. "Figures I couldn't get an easy answer to that. Alright, well, we have a clearer timeline of what he was doing and who he saw in the past week. I've got some holes to fill, but not many. The newspaper ad I put out asking for information helped. We've been filtering through people off and on all morning. I expect more to show up this afternoon and tomorrow."

At this moment, all information helped. Although... oh dear. That meant I had to talk with even more people, didn't it? I bit back a sigh before it could escape. What were the odds I could convince Jamie that I once again had some magical aspect of the case requiring my utmost concentration, leaving the witnesses to her?

Yes, I was well aware I was doomed. No need to rub it in.

squeak, squeak

What in magic's name are you doing?

rubbing it in

Why are we friends again?

Like I said before, you're a glutton for punishment. I don't know what else to tell you.

Report 13: Speed

You're an adrenaline addict.

and your point is....

Made.

There always comes a point where the case stalls for a bit. We hit that a day later. All the witnesses we could find were interviewed, the requested records for Burtchell's finances weren't in yet, and we didn't have any other leads to follow. Burtchell's funeral was set for two days later, and Henri was whining about not having enough clean clothes, so we decided to temporarily pack up and retreat to Kingston for a well-deserved weekend off.

For some reason, I got vetoed about driving back, Sherard taking the wheel instead. I settled in the back with Henri and Clint, Penny taking shotgun. We headed back to Kingston at a crawling twenty-five miles an hour. Why were people in this culture so afraid of speed? Seriously, they were terrified of going over thirty. I kept debunking stupid rumor after stupider old wives' tale and it was driving me to drink. Didn't they understand we could get to other places *much faster* without risking life and limb?

I'd beat this into them or die trying.

As we trundled back toward the capital, Penny turned in her seat to ask me, "Why did you request his finances? You think this might be due to a gambling problem after all?"

"It's very much a longshot," I admitted with spread hands. "But motive for murder usually boils down to money, power, love, or revenge. He wasn't having any affairs with married women, or had any romantic entanglements at all that we can tell. So love is out. He was a retired royal mage out in the country, so power is out. All we have left is money and revenge."

"His finances seemed in good order, though," Henri objected. "No one's suggested he was being chased by bill collectors."

"Which is why it's a longshot. Most gamblers eventually have problems with owing the wrong people, but Burtchell seemed one of those rare few who was in control of his vice. On the surface, anyway. I want a complete record of his finances to see if that was really true or not. At this point, any lead to follow, you know?"

"We do indeed." Sherard didn't take his eyes off the road as he addressed me. "And when that lead fizzles out? Because I have a hunch it will."

"Well," I sighed, "that is the question, isn't it?"

The trip back killed me slowly because of the crawling speed—really, on a bike, I'd have been there in half the time—but the ride itself was fun. Henri was in rare form, joking and messing with people. Penny was giving back as good as she got, and Sherard seemed to enjoy tweaking everyone's noses. The only problem I had was keeping Clint inside the vehicle. He thought it a grand idea to climb up top and sunbathe on the roof. He was likely hungry. His source of food was the sun, and he'd been napping inside the hotel for the past twenty or so hours.

"I believe we'd have proven our theory faster if we had someone aside from Davenforth firing the bullets," Sherard teased with a challenging grin and a waggle of the eyebrows that would have done Bugs Bunny proud. "With all due respect, your marksmanship leaves *much* to be desired."

'All due respect' was a wonderful expression because it didn't specify how much respect was actually due. Could be none.

Henri apparently went with none, as he retorted, "Sir, if I am to be insulted, I must value your opinion. Besides, you weren't doing any better. Who kept hitting outside the target and clipping off the board's corners?"

"I was still working on the appropriate amount of force more than trajectory when I did that!" Sherard argued cheerfully.

"That explains the first two missing corners, certainly, but what about the rest of the board?"

"Oh, like *you* have room to talk. At least I hit the board consistently!"

"You say that as if I didn't. I'll have you know, I wasn't aiming at thin air. Your aim is so atrocious I feared for my own safety."

I rolled my eyes heavenward. Were they twelve? "Okay, stop. You're meandering into the realms of absurdity right now."

"Sorry," Henri apologized. He crossed his arms over his chest, signaling an end to the argument.

"And where is my apology?" Sherard demanded.

"It could not be located," Henri shot back.

I snorted a laugh as they got right back into it. Really, these two. Any chance to rib each other, and they'd take it. They loved to tease each other almost as much as they enjoyed working with each other. It made me wonder, though. What would it have been like for Henri if I'd never met him?

Not to suggest he didn't have friends—he did—but he was such an introvert by nature that he didn't think to suggest social activities. He needed Sherard and I, the extroverts, to pull him out of his comfortable routines. And I had a feeling this world would have suffered a bit if they hadn't met. These two were a formidable match and would come up with some ingenious things working together.

It was what gave me hope they'd figure out Belladonna's portal spells eventually. I knew I couldn't go home—I was resigned to that. Sad, because I missed family and friends, and sometimes I still got homesick. But I understood going home wasn't a possibility for me.

Still, it'd be great if I could send word back somehow. Tell people I was alive and well, and to not grieve for me. I knew Henri and Sherard were still mulling over the information they'd learned. They might not have said much to me about it for fear of raising my hopes, but neither man gave up a challenge easily. I chose to have faith in their collective genius.

We arrived at the station back in Kingston but headed inside only long enough to carry in Henri's equipment. Then we all went our separate ways, heading for home. Well, Henri and I caught a taxi together to save on cab fare.

I lounged back in the taxi's seat, legs propped up against the opposite door. There wasn't really enough room for the posture, but my butt was numb after four hours on a seat that wasn't really well sprung. I couldn't handle sitting properly just now. Clint used my legs to stand on so he could brace his front paws on the window and poke his head outside, watching the cars and people as they went by. Henri was slouched on the opposite side in much the same posture, his hat on the bench next to him.

"I would like to say that in my absence someone has handled the routine magical casework at the station." Henri said this in the most deadpan tone ever delivered by a human being.

"You could say that," I agreed in a similar tone. "You'd be wrong, but you could say it."

"I find myself very frustrated. On the one hand, we have a near impossible case to solve. On the other, I have work stacking up with no possibility of me attending to it in the near future."

I nodded in empathy, sharing the frustration. We all felt the frustration. Our work didn't go away or solve itself just because we were out of town investigating another case. A policeman's work was never done. I could only hope for a break soon, a lead that would give us the edge we needed.

The taxi pulled up to the curb and we clambered out. I paid the driver while Henri went for our bags, tied on the back of the taxi. He had them levitated and up the stairs before I noticed what he was doing.

"I'll drop yours off at your door," he called over his shoulder.

It was on the tip of my tongue to refuse this offer. Henri tended to bump into things when he used levitation spells on stairways, and he'd already dinged one wall in this apartment building. Plus, I was perfectly capable of carrying my own suitcase, even without Belladonna's enhancements.

But I knew better than to step on a man's pride, and it was a sweet gesture on his part. I smiled and let him go. "Sure."

The door opened under his hand and swung inwards, revealing Mrs. Henderson. She looked frazzled, wispies sticking out in every direction instead of her usual sleek, greying bun. On seeing us, she lit up in relief. To be more accurate, on seeing Clint she lit up in relief. "Oh, you're home again, dears. The case solved, then?"

"No, we came back in town for a funeral," I corrected her. Well able to read the expression on her face, I asked wryly, "Mice playing while the cat's away?"

"I'm afraid so. Clint, honey, would you...?"

Clint was already looking about him, nose and ears flickering as he searched out his future victims. He paused to reassure her seriously, "I'll hunt."

Mrs. Henderson practically beamed down at him. "Thank you, dear. I hear them in the pantry for the most part."

He bounded immediately for her ground floor apartment without even a by-your-leave, the traitor. I shook my head and let him play. He'd been good the entire trip in and was likely anxious to stretch out.

I let him go, following Henri upstairs. "So, what are you going to do the rest of the day?"

"I have a book I haven't finished and a large tub."

Soak and read, huh? It did sound nice, but I was too ant-
sy to do something like lounge around the apartment for the
rest of the day. "I suppose you'll finish off a box of chocolates
while you're relaxing."

He stopped on the second story landing and gave me a
fishy glower. "I have no chocolates in my flat."

I busted out laughing. "Liar. The day you don't have
chocolate is the day the world ends. It's fine, I'll leave your
stash alone."

"Chance would be a fine thing," he groused before continuing up.

I stopped him at the third landing and gestured for him to
release my bag. "I can go the last leg. You're tired, go soak."

"Are you certain?" He looked strangely reluctant to part,
a feeling I shared. But we'd been basically in each other's
pockets for days now, so I suppose it made sense. "Well, of
course, I shouldn't question your strength."

"That you should not," I agreed lightly. I took the suitcase in hand and gave him an analyst's salute. "Enjoy your
book."

I hauled my suitcase upstairs, changed into something less
formal, and went promptly back out again. I had no food
in the house and I wanted lunch. It felt strange to be alone,
though. That feeling hadn't passed. I wanted company, but
not enough to pull Henri out of his apartment. He likely
needed a little 'me' time after being with people nonstop for
a week. Introverts needed time to recharge. I could respect
that.

Who else could I invite out? The answer came to me as
soon as I asked the question, and I paused in the stairwell to
message Ellie: *Back in town. Lunch?*

She responded promptly: *Where?*

Amelia's on Fourth?

Meet you there in twenty.

Perfect. I wanted to run the car's performance past her,
give her some ideas of what needed to change in order to
make it more stable. And maybe run the idea of a motorcycle

past her as well. If I didn't have passengers, no one could complain about my speed, right?

I couldn't make myself get back into a car today, though, and really there was no need. Amelia's was only a few blocks down anyway. I enjoyed the summer air and the bustle of the city as I walked the distance.

Miss Amelia's Bakery was as heavenly in scent as usual. She was most known for her pastries—for good reason—but she did offer a lunch menu as well. I breathed in deeply as I entered through the front door, the shop bell ringing out merrily as I stepped across the threshold. Clam chowder and an iced tea were definitely on my mind.

I'd barely put in my order and settled at a window table when Ellie blew through like a summer typhoon. My friend was a little intense when she had projects on the brain. Ellie went straight to the counter, put in her own order for food, then blazed toward me, green eyes alight with an almost unholy fervor. "How is it? Did it work?"

"Did fifty miles an hour for ten minutes without straining the engine," I reported with immense satisfaction.

Ellie threw up a fist, punching the air in victory. She dropped into the chair so heavily that even with her petite build, she almost sent it crashing down. Was that a streak of oil against her fair skin? Ha, it sure was. And she had no less than three drafting pencils stuck in her messy red hair, caging it in a loose bun. Caught her mid-project, did I? "*Yes!* Why did you stop there?"

"Couple of problems." I ticked them off on my fingers. "Road was too slick from the recent rain. I wasn't getting enough traction; the tires couldn't handle it. Suspension wasn't up to the task either, so we got jostled pretty badly. And third, Henri was in the car."

She snorted at that last point. "That man has no sense of adventure."

"Tell me about it."

"But suspension and tires…" She trailed off, eyes narrowed. "I think we can do something about those. You mentioned before the tires on Earth are wider."

"Much wider. A good six inches wider, in fact."

"Hmm. I can see how that would help with traction and stability. You have time today?"

That was Ellie code speak for: You have time to invent with me today? "Sure. Actually, come to that, Ellie. There's something I want you to build for me."

Her expression lit up hopefully. "Yes?"

"You know that thing I mentioned before, the motorcycle?"

"Oh, yes, yes, is it time to tinker with that? Please tell me it is, I keep thinking of different designs, but you barely gave me a basic description."

"I want the option of going somewhere without taking all year to get there, so yes, definitely time to build it."

She chortled like a demented dragon with the promise of gold. This woman, I swear. Talk about a one-track mind.

"I've only got today and tomorrow to help you with the initial design," I warned her. "We're not done with the case yet."

Ellie blinked at me in surprise. "I assumed since you were back, you'd solved it."

I groaned, head hanging for a moment. "I wish. We're basically stalled at this point. It's a locked-room murder mystery. We can't figure out how the murderer got in or out, since the wards are still intact and the keys in the house. We have a timeline of that morning, and it's unbelievably tight, but no one saw anyone suspicious. We've barely figured out *how* Burtchell was killed—even that wasn't conventional. I have literally never seen a case so strange."

"And that's saying something," she remarked. We both paused as our food arrived, set in front of us by a smiling waitress. After she retreated, Ellie continued, "But really? You have both RM Seaton and Henri, and they can't figure out how an intruder slipped through the wards?"

"Trust me, it's driving them up the wall. I'm actually glad I had an excuse to drag them away from it for two days. They keep banging their heads against that particular problem."

"What was your excuse?"

"Burtchell's funeral is on Gather Day. We all needed fresh clothes and a day off, so we came back in."

"Ah." She dipped into her lunch with a moan of bliss. "I do love this bakery."

"Tell me about it." I ate mine with similar gusto, more than a little hungry.

We fell to discussing motorcycles, and tires, and suspensions. I'd worked summers at my uncle's garage growing up, and while I didn't know everything about cars, I knew a bit more than the average Joe. I could at least describe the basics of the parts, what they looked like and how they generally functioned. It kept Ellie from shooting blindly into the dark.

After lunch, we retreated to her place and put designs onto paper. I lost all sense of time as we worked. That was often the case. Ellie was the type who was so enthusiastic about a project, her attitude swept you along with her. It felt much like being caught in a riptide sometimes.

And look at me, making sea analogies. I'd turn native yet.

With the hope of a motorcycle in my near future, I had a spring in my step as I walked back to the apartment. Clint lounged on the front stoop, clearly waiting for me, his ears flicking back and forth idly as he picked up and dismissed the ambient sounds around him. I leaned down and scooped him up, cradling the warm weight of him against my chest. "And did you find Mrs. Henderson's naughty mouse?"

He purred in smug satisfaction. "Mouse gone."

"What a good kitty you are. Want some clean water?"

"Mrs. Henderson give some."

"Of course she did." I shook my head in amusement as I carried him up. "Clint, did you like going with me to work the case?"

He brightened, practically bristling. "Yes. Go again?"

"About that; would you like to? You were very helpful, reaching areas that were hard for me to go. Henri said if we train you right, he'd think you can help on some of the cases."

Clint nodded like a puppet with its string cut. "Yes, yes, train. Go."

And that answered that question. "After this case, we'll think of all you can do, okay?"

"Okay, okay."

I'd heard of field dogs, but field cats? This had to be one for the records.

I pattered around my apartment, getting ready to turn in for the night. It was late enough that I didn't sing in the shower, as I was wont to do, not wanting to disturb my neighbors. I hummed a variety of songs instead, whatever suited my mood. Clint was passed out on the bed by the time I climbed into PJ's, and I just rolled him over so I had room to get in. I snuggled into my pillow and sighed with contentment. It didn't matter how comfortable a hotel might be, you always missed your own bed.

It had been a full day, so I dropped to sleep fairly quickly. I fell into dreamland, in a deep sleep, utterly relaxed and happy to be there.

The next thing I knew, I bolted upright, the thought clamoring through my head like a fire station's alarm.

I knew how he'd gotten in.

Swearing, I threw back the covers, jostling Clint in the process. He gave a sleepy growl at me, but I didn't pause. Throwing on a robe and slippers, I sprinted down the stairs like a madwoman for the floor right below mine. Some part of my brain cautioned me to be quiet—it was birds' hours of the morning—but I could barely restrain myself, I was so excited. It was a miracle I kept my knock on Henri's door down to a polite rap of the knuckles. I wanted to throw the door open like some dojo challenger.

I could hear him grumble and fuss as he got up, the heavy pad of his feet as he stumbled to the door. He jerked it open with one eye shut, the other barely focused, his dark curls in a snarl from his pillow, and the crease of sleep against one cheek. He would've looked adorable if he hadn't had the attitude of a wounded grizzly. "Wha?"

I shoved past him, closing the door behind me, still vibrating. "Henri. I know how he did it. I know how the murderer got in and out of the house."

He went from sleepy to alert in two seconds. "How?!"

"Think about it. What was the one section of the house no one was in, for a whole half hour of time?"

His brows compressed but he wasn't awake enough to really think. Or he was still stuck on the wards, either way. The answer wasn't coming, even with that hint.

Taking pity, I started at the beginning. "I don't think the murderer had to take down the wards, or duplicate a key, or any of the complex situations we considered. I think it was timing and stealth on his part. Think about the timeline. The postman and milkman both said the front doors were open when they made their deliveries. Villarreal was talking to Burtchell in the study when the postman was there. As much activity as the front door was getting, no one really entered the house. I think the killer snuck in between those deliveries, while Burtchell was visiting with his friend. He went straight up the stairs to lie in wait until everyone was gone. It was safe to do that—no one had gone upstairs all morning, not until the constables arrived and searched the house."

Now Henri was awake. He finished the thought in growing excitement. "He waits, Villarreal leaves, he comes down. Kills Burtchell. Can't find the key so goes back upstairs. The housekeeper comes in not ten minutes later, finds her dead employer, runs out of the house to fetch help. All he has to do is leave. She didn't lock the doors behind her."

I beamed at him, still bouncing on my toes. "See? It's not a locked room mystery at all! It just looked that way on the surface."

"Oh, this man is very clever." Henri rubbed his hands together absently, a light in his eye that promised retribution. He got like that when he finally caught a criminal's scent. He was part bloodhound, I swear. "How long did he watch Burtchell to get his routine down like this? Or did he just see an opportunity to slip through the defenses and took it?"

"Could be a mix of both. I'd think, though, if he were that determined to kill a royal mage, he'd spend at least some time planning and watching him to figure out how to get to him."

"It makes sense to me as well." Henri stepped in, put both arms around my waist and hugged me tightly.

I was so surprised by this I nearly didn't hug him back. He was usually so uptight with his rules about proper conduct I could never really get a proper hug out of him. This problem must have been really stressing him out.

"Thank you, bless your brain," he said against my temple. "I'm so glad you figured this out. I was about to lose what's left of my sanity."

"You're welcome." I grinned against his ear.

Pulling free, he retreated two steps. "Let's call Seaton."

"At this hour of the morning?" I objected.

He gave me a baleful glare for some reason. "You have no issue with jerking me out of a peaceful slumber, but you don't wish to awake him?"

I thought about that for a full microsecond. "You make a good point. You want to explain it, or do I?"

"Oh, by all means, go right ahead. It's your accomplishment, after all."

I skipped over to where his telephone sat on its small little table, dialing in the number for Sherard's upscale townhouse.

It rang for a solid two minutes before someone growled into the receiver, *"Whoever this is, there better be an emergency. Interrupting a royal mage's sleep is a corporal punishment."*

I'd forgotten. Sherard was not a morning person. Oh well. "Good morning, Sunshine!"

"Jamie." A gusty sigh. *"Are you ill?"*

"I'm calling with good news, not bad."

"Unless I've won the lottery, I don't care. Leave me alone."

Really not a morning person. "So you're saying that how

the murderer got in and out of the house isn't important to you?"

There was a beat of silence. "*Start talking.*"

I grinned. That was more like it.

revelation have waited

Although really, couldn't this revelation have waited until after breakfast?

Now where's the fun in that?

Report 14: Four for a Funeral

The funeral of a royal mage, even one retired, was quite the spectacle. I'd more or less expected as much and braced myself accordingly. Jamie, I believe, was not as well-prepared for the event. She kept looking about her with a bemused air and wide brown eyes.

It was a refreshing change to see her in a dress, even one the pure white of mourning. Actually, the brightness of it set off her golden skin and hair in a very flattering manner. With her hair done up in a proper updo, pearls dangling from her ears, she looked the part of a society lady instead of the woman famous for killing a rogue witch. It made me wish I could take her on a more social function, something without the solemn, depressed air that surrounded us now. It was an odd feeling. I disliked social events as a norm, but I knew she enjoyed them. And escorting her here depressed the spirits.

The coffin trundled past us on a flatbed wagon, pulled by a matching pair of white horses. A regiment of kingsmen in full dress uniform followed in its wake. Every gentleman doffed his hat as the wagon passed by. The paved road to the cemetery was filled on both sides, several rows deep, but eerily silent considering the hundreds of people packed into the space. The younger onlookers seemed grim but there out of obligation, much as we were. The older generation had more than a few tears in their eyes. It only made sense. They were the ones who knew Burtchell best— he had been *their* royal mage, the one who'd served that generation.

I watched the crowd, thinking of what would happen

if we didn't solve this case, didn't find the murderer. The public outcry would be ferocious. It gave me chills just envisioning it.

Seaton was further up in the crowd, at the royal family's side during all this. McSparrin was supposedly here as well—she'd stated her intentions to attend— but I'd not yet spotted her. I might not have seen Jamie if we hadn't come in the same cab. It was deucedly crowded anywhere near the graveyard.

Despite the casting of several voice amplification spells, I only caught part of the eulogy. The wind was strong enough that it caught and snatched the words, whisking them away from my ears. Queen Regina kept it brief, I think because she feared she'd keep us here for days otherwise, talking of the man. The kingsmen set off a military salute, guns firing in unison seven times. Then Seaton and his royal mage counterparts stepped forward and lit up the cloudy summer day with a breathtaking display of fireworks that turned the sky alight like a second sun. I'd not seen anything in my life that could begin to compare to it.

The coffin was lowered into the ground as the fireworks raged on, and people were allowed to approach and throw in flowers, letters, or other tokens. The funeral was more or less over at that point. I turned to the woman at my side and asked softly, "Ices and an early lunch?"

"Heavens, yes." Jamie accepted the elbow I extended, walking steadily at my side as we gently bullied our way free of the crowd. She leaned her head in to say quietly against my ear, "It's such a sad thing, seeing this. He was very loved."

The loss of any life was a sad thing to me. If nothing else, I mourned the loss of potential. Even with criminals, I could see the path they could have walked, the ones they chose to ignore. It was a different sort of sadness. This was possibly the worst display I'd seen yet of how much it affected everyone when a life was cut short. "I empathize completely. Even retired, he did much good in the world. Truly, he was a royal mage by heart and not just calling."

"I keep thinking, the motive behind his murder must be the key. If we can just unlock that, we'd understand the whole picture. Right now we only have pieces, and they don't fit well enough together for me to properly see what I'm looking for." She sighed in frustration.

Finally passing the cemetery's main gates, we found a little breathing room by ducking to the side, walking along the bordering sidewalk. A long line trailed in from the other side, preventing us from walking the direction we actually needed to go. We'd have to go up a block and around them.

As we walked, Jamie fell into a pensive silence. I let her stew for a moment, for I knew that look. I'd not been acquainted with her long before I'd learned to recognize it. When her eyes narrowed just so, her brows quirked together, she was thinking hard about something. It was the way she kept lifting her hand to her mouth, as if to bite at her thumbnail, only to pull it back down again that truly gave it away. I had the distinct impression she'd been a terrible nail biter in her youth. She'd broken the habit as an adult, but it took willpower on her end to remember to not indulge the bad habit.

We paused at a street corner, waiting for traffic to pass before stepping across. She must have sensed my regard as she stopped, thinking long enough to look at me askance. "What?"

"You tell me, you're the one thinking so hard."

Pulling a face, she admitted, "I just have this gut feeling I can't explain away. Cop's instincts, I guess. I think the motive behind Burtchell's death is revenge."

It was truly curious, the paths her mind took. "Why

so?"

"Okay, hear me out. We know people loved and adored Burtchell—we've been hearing nothing else—but no one can be universally loved. He was getting some flack about not saving all those ships, right? Even though the people writing him recanted their first letters, you still had the angry ones. It proves my point, he couldn't live as long as he did, as such a powerful man, without making a few enemies. We didn't find anything in Sheffield, but he'd not lived there for long, either. A few years. Maybe this ties back to something he did while he was still in Kingston."

I followed her train of thought well enough—or thought I did. "And the reason for the delay in killing Burtchell is because this person was incarcerated? Or somehow detained in a manner that kept him or her from reaching Burtchell until recently?"

"Maybe after Burtchell retired, the murderer wasn't sure where he went." Jamie shrugged, her free hand splayed. "It wasn't like he was listed in any public phone book. Not that you people have many of those to begin with. It wasn't until that bad storm, when he saved the ships, that he made national headlines."

"Which would give his location away." I had to admit, it made a certain amount of sense. "It gives us a wider suspect pool, to be sure. It'll mean combing through his cases, whatever he worked on before he retired."

Jamie deadpanned, "Yay, more archive digging."

"Might I remind you this is your idea?"

"It doesn't mean I have to be happy with my idea. Even if I think it's the only path forward. You know we can't leave this one unsolved. There will be a riot."

"Yes, truly." I saw a taxi pull to the curb with a vacant sign popped up on top of the roof and flagged it down. If I didn't have to walk in this muggy, abominably hot weather, all the better. "Then I suppose after lunch we should change and get back to work. It'll take the course of several days to research everything and track people down."

She pointed a finger at me, her tone accusing, as if denouncing me as an axe murderer. "You like research projects."

"I like sleeping in my own bed every night," I sassed back.

Rolling her eyes at me, she accepted my hand to help her up into the taxi. "Of course. I should have realized that was your motivation."

"Naturally."

Seaton heard us out later that day. He was still in full dress uniform, toned down from his customary flamboyancy, and much more somber than usual. He leaned against the edge of Jamie's desk as she explained her theory, taking it in with only the occasional nod.

"I might be able to save us from digging," he finally stated after a thoughtful pause. "As it happens, Weiss stopped me on the way out. He's demanding to be let into the investigation. This seems a good way for him to help."

Weiss? Weiss, as in the head of the kingsmen? Great magic, but that seemed a bit over the top, to call in a man like that for a murder investigation. Then again, he'd been in the kingsmen for the past three decades. If anyone knew of all the skeletons hidden in the closets, it would likely be him. "I'm for it. He might know half of the answers we need just off the top of his head. If nothing else, he'll know where to look."

Jamie nodded in agreement, although a trifle dubiously. "Are you sure about this, though, Sherard?

Weiss doesn't really like me."

I did a double take. "Come again?"

Seaton grimaced in a mix of agreement and some consternation. "It's not that, it's more he didn't trust you at first. Your story was pretty wild. And then he was afraid you were a magical ticking bomb. Which, to be fair, you rather were until I figured out how to stabilize you. He's sort of revised his opinion of you since then. At least, he thinks you're not a danger to the country."

"High praise," she drawled.

I wasn't sure how to take this report. Then again, I knew Weiss only by reputation, having never crossed paths with the man before. He was of the old guard, and that might mean certain prejudices about a woman being a detective, as well. I did not care for it when men made unnecessary judgements about my partner. I cared for it even less when they chose to voice their asinine opinions. If he was of that type, I didn't care how helpful he could be, I'd give him the boot. If Jamie didn't do it herself, naturally. Only fair I give her first dibs.

Jamie looked as if she were being fed rotten fish with a side of spoiled lemons, but she grudgingly gave Seaton the go-ahead. "Call him in. Tell him what we're looking for. We'll start in the morning, I guess."

"We'll need to meet at the Kingsmen Archives. Only place all this information is stored." Seaton stopped using the desk as a prop and straightened both cuffs with a negligent twitch of his hands, an idle tic. "I thought we could take a moment and renew your spells while we both are here."

"Oh, sure." Jamie popped out of her desk chair and followed him into a nearby conference room.

I watched them go with a frown. That was still something we needed to solve. Having to redo Jamie's spells every month was ridiculous in the extreme.

Surely what one madwoman had created, two saner magicians could unravel. Surely.

Only a few hours remained of the workday, so I thought to retreat to my lab and see if there was something I could do to help with the workload. I wouldn't be of much use in the upcoming days, and I felt rather bad for the other magical examiner in the station. The man had barely started a month ago and already he was having to take up not only my slack but Sanderson's.

I'd barely gotten settled at the table when I heard a rap of knuckles at the door. Looking up, I was surprised to see my captain in the doorway. We'd already given him a brief report of our progress. What was he here for? "Captain Gregson. Something wrong?"

He came in and shut the door behind him, an unreadable expression on his face. I'd only seen that expression at a card table or when he was grappling with something of a political nature. His gravelly voice was a touch deeper as he spoke. "Davenforth. Level with me. Did you get RM Seaton to write a report against Sanderson, asking for his dismissal?"

Ah. I'd wondered when that would come back around to me. "I did not. Frankly? I didn't need to. Seaton saw Sanderson in full form during our last case. He was...less than pleased with the man's conduct and work ethics."

Gregson let out a pent-up breath, shoulders relaxing from the unnatural stiffness he'd entered with. He looked as if he'd run his hands repeatedly through his grey hair. It stuck up in short spikes, a sign of stress on his part. His suit was also in disarray, the tie missing, and I could only think he'd yanked it off, another sign of stress.

This question on his part had weight to it, and I paid even closer attention. "Thank all deities. I know you hate the man, and he's given you good cause for it, but I can't condone people going behind my back and pulling political strings to deal with problematic colleagues. I didn't think you had—you're always a straight shooter about this sort of thing—but I had to ask."

I waved away the semi-apology. "Understandable. What's happened?"

"Well, RM Seaton's report hit all the right desks. I say right, because he went far above the commissioner's head. He didn't mince words, either. He made it very clear that having a man that bigoted and lazy was a detriment to any department and Sanderson shouldn't be in a police force at all, at any station. The commissioner is now backpedaling and defending his decision to ignore multiple letters, recriminations, and complaints about Sanderson over the past six years. In that respect, I thank you. Having that thick of a paper trail, showing how incompetent the man is, backs up RM Seaton's stance quite nicely."

I smirked. It wasn't a nice expression, I'm sure. "Anything to be of assistance. Do I dare hope we'll finally be shed of the idiot?"

"Odds are very favorable right now, I'll say that. The commissioner keeps talking about demoting him, or reassigning him, but every time he's come in to talk to me about it, I've turned the tables on him. I record the conversation as best I can on paper and then go above his head to report it. It's all very politicky, but it's getting results." Gregson paused and with unholy glee admitted, "We might get a new commissioner at this rate."

I sat back with a huff of astonishment. "Over Sanderson?!"

"It's not really that, I don't think. Or I should say, Sanderson might be the lynchpin that topples the whole stack. Because the commissioner has so steadfastly protected him, manipulating records even to do it, it's called into light what *else* he might have done. Who else he's protected when he shouldn't have. The Powers That Be aren't sounding too thrilled with him at the moment."

Gregson looked outright gleeful over this prospect. I must say, I shared his enthusiasm. The commissioner had been a thorn in my side in regard to Sanderson, which was the only reason why I personally disliked the idiot. So it seemed petty to wish for his dismissal. Gregson, however, had many reasons to complain about the man. His stance was far more justified.

Clearing his throat, Gregson continued, "One more thing. I wanted to catch you and Edwards apart and get your responses to this separately. There's some talk about you and Edwards becoming consultants for the kingsmen."

I blinked at him, quite certain I'd misheard. "I'm sorry?"

"Queen Regina was very impressed with your results of the last case," he explained. "And she's pleased with your progress on this case."

"We haven't found the murderer yet," I objected, not following this at all.

"She apparently has complete faith you will. I don't think the offer hinges upon the results of this case, per se, but it might. When she was in here to request you as investigators, she spoke to me of it. I think she's realized that while her kingsmen are quite effective in what they do, they have blind spots in their training and experience. And between me and you, she likes having Jamie in the limelight as a female detective. An *effective* female detective."

Yes, of course, I should have seen it. Queen Regina was campaigning hard for women to be seen with the same value as men in every working field. She already regarded Jamie favorably. Of course she'd want my partner to be the poster child for this. "Jamie I understand, but why me?"

"She likes you." Gregson shrugged. "Our good queen adores the competent, and you've shown yourself to be that. That, and I think she might have tried sounding Edwards out before, about doing this and Edwards flat refused to go without you."

I flushed a bit, my cheeks heating, and I rubbed at them to hide it, glancing away. Jamie made no secret of how she loved working with me. I adored having her as a partner just as much. In truth, if she went somewhere, I'd likely follow.

"Davenforth, let's be clear on this. You can be consultants for the kingsmen, that's fine, but you can't leave." Gregson shook a finger at me sternly, belying the twinkle in his eyes. "I'm not losing the partnership with the highest close rate to those Red Men."

I snorted at the kingsmen's nickname, amused to hear the slang out of my respectable captain's mouth. "Understood, sir. I have no doubt if Jamie hears about this offer, she'll be inclined to take it. She has close ties to them, as you're aware. I think she'd revel in the chance to work with them. And I don't...that is, I don't wish to lose her as a partner."

He seemed to expect this answer, and the smugness on his face was entirely ridiculous. "This from the man who objected he didn't want a partner at all."

"Yes, yes, you were right, I was wrong. Satisfied?"

"Immensely." He had the audacity to grin at me. "I'll speak with Edwards about what she wants to do."

I felt it only fair to warn him. "Are you quite certain we won't be stepping on toes? I understand Kingsman Weiss dislikes Jamie."

Gregson's head jerked in surprise. "Now that I hadn't heard. You sure?"

"Both Seaton and Jamie spoke of it earlier."

"Oh. Well now, that sheds a different light on things, doesn't it? If Queen Regina put forth the idea, she can definitely override Weiss, but Edwards might not wish to take the offer if she has to work with a superior who hates her. Hmm. Still, I'll run it by her. It's entirely her choice."

Was it really, though? A queen had made the offer.

Well, maybe Seaton was right and Weiss had changed his attitude toward Jamie. If that were the case, then my worry was rather moot, wasn't it?

Report 15: The Archives

I entered the Kingsmen Archives with a mixed feeling of dread and resignation. I'd been in here a few times, although Henri informed me it was his first foray into this labyrinthine place. I've always thought of the Archives as a mix between *Beauty and the Beast*'s library and the *Labyrinth*. Or maybe it was more *Alice in Wonderland*. The place was massive, full of doors and hallways, and any door you chose either opened into a musty, sunless room of books or some magical portal. Rumor had it at least a dozen interns had disappeared since the place opened a hundred years ago. Frankly, I believed it.

Sherard was our guide, leading ahead and flicking on magic lights as he moved. He was still in a somber mood, as he had been since the news of Burtchell's murder. He'd taken it harder than I'd expected. Clearly, the two men were closer than I'd assumed. But he was also pulling himself out of the funk, processing through the stages of grief. He'd gone through denial. Was he at anger yet?

Glancing back, our guide asked, "Why did you bring Clint?"

I carefully didn't shrug or disrupt the cat perched on my shoulder. "He's good at pattern recognition. I figure, teach him the words to look out for, and he'll be able to help comb through the records."

Clint groomed a paw before saying in his high tenor, "I work cat."

"Field cat," I corrected him in amusement. "It's called a field cat, darling. You do work, though."

"And why is he perched on your shoulder?" Penny asked in amusement.

"Because he was a parrot in a previous life." I flicked this away in a casual gesture. "What I want to know is, why are we here? I thought Weiss was going to give us the down-low on possible suspects."

"And so I am." Weiss took one step around a ceiling-high bookcase and paused there like a menacing specter.

I didn't jump out of my skin, although it was a near thing. My senses were heightened—nose, ears, sight, everything by a good twenty-two percent. And Weiss *still* managed to sneak up on me on a regular basis. I wasn't really convinced he was human. Ghost, maybe. The way he moved through places without seemingly any connection, I half-expected him to don a white mask and start belting out "Phantom of the Opera."

Penny and Henri, I noticed, both startled. Sherard didn't. Then again, Sherard was probably immune to Weiss after so many years.

"Seaton." Weiss's flinty grey eyes swept him from head to toe, his thin mouth quirking down in an unhappy manner. "You are your usual self, I see."

It was true Sherard was back in his usual flamboyant red coat, which flared dramatically around his calves, his white shirt with a ruffled and lacy collar all starched within an inch of its life. The guyliner was in place for the first time in days. It's how I knew he'd worked himself out of his initial shock. He'd been far too somberly dressed for most of the case so far. It was good to see him in his usual theatrical getup.

Sherard regarded Weiss levelly, not at all flustered by this semi-accusation. "Rather than mourn him, I'd prefer to avenge him."

For the first time in history, Weiss stopped frowning severely and looked almost—shock, gasp!—approving for a split second. "My sentiments exactly. Well. Perhaps my aid won't be a lost cause after all. Who're these other two?"

As if the man didn't know that very well. I gritted my teeth and made the introductions. "This is my partner, Dr. Henri Davenforth. He's a magical examiner. And this is Officer Penny McSparrin. Everyone, Archibald Weiss, Kingsmen Commander.""

He gave them nothing more than a curt nod before his eyes went straight to Clint. "You brought a pet in here?"

I had my mouth open on a hot retort, but Henri beat me to it.

"She brought a magician's familiar, a Felix, in here. I believe that's acceptable." Henri made it clear by tone alone that if he wanted to buy that fight, Henri would certainly sell it.

It bemused me, really. Henri was usually this easy-going gentleman, but man, if he did get pissed off? He was like a wounded badger. I don't think he knows the whole idiom of 'float like a butterfly, sting like a bee.' He was all bee.

Sherard also got impatient about Weiss's attitude, I could see it in the dark glare he gave the man. "Quite. A familiar is not denied anywhere. Now, can we get on with it, Weiss?"

Weiss harrumphed—I didn't know people actually did that in real life—and spun on his heel like a damsel ready to flee a party over a ripped dress. Dramatic, much? We had to stretch our legs to keep up with him. He led the way to a small sitting area with a table, six chairs, and a few lamps nearby. A study niche, I assumed.

He didn't sit, just paused, his fingertips grazing the table as he faced us frostily, his chin up at an arrogant angle. "I believe there were several cases that meet your qualifications. I've made a preemptive list of the most recent ones. Of those cases, we'll need to search the records and see if the convicted persons match the qualities of the murderer and whether they were at liberty to commit it."

Yes, thank you, it's not like we don't know what we're all doing here. Could I stab him yet? I had a cat I could fling at his face, that might be satisfying. Clint would totally go for it. His fur was bristled along his spine, and while he wasn't Halloween kitty yet, he was getting there.

"The archivist is on hand and I have another agent standing by at the prison to check records for us. I hope to go through this as quickly as possible," Weiss continued with un-ruffled calm.

Well at least he was efficient. You had to give him that.

We pulled the records, some of them case books. Like, the actual notes taken during a case. The archivist helpfully set them in the middle of the table and we all took a seat, randomly divvying out the pile. It really didn't matter who took what. I cracked open one of the case books and just barely managed to keep a groan of dismay behind my teeth. It was hard enough on most days for me to read this country's very confusing language, but add in the spidery chicken scratch Burtchell used? I felt like stabbing my eyes out.

The book was abruptly nudged out of my hands, another file sliding in over top of it. I gave Henri a grateful look, which he returned with a wink, and went back to reading. Or trying to. I did take a moment to study my familiar in amusement. Clint had propped open one of the files, his back leg stretched out to hold the flap open, and used a dainty paw to flip through the pages. "Clint, you still good with what words to search for?"

"Burtchell, murder, kill, threat, prison, revenge," the cat recited precisely. "Fish."

"I think that last one is a Clint addition," Sherard snickered from across the table. "Look at sentence time too. Here." He scratched out three words on a piece of paper and flipped it around, sliding it toward Clint. "If it says any of these three, set it aside. It's not what we need."

I leaned in towards my furry friend to read over the top of his head. *Lifetime* and *no parole*. Yeah, those were good additions. If we knew the prisoner was still in, no use looking him up.

Weiss frowned at all the talking and harrumphed again. I ignored him. The man was so very old school that he wanted all work, no chitchat. But you know, not only did chitchat bleed off tension in stressful cases like this, it often sparked ideas. How could you know what the other person did if you didn't communicate it? Needless to say, I didn't agree with him.

Silence fell as we skimmed through the records. Really, I was looking for proper motive. Weiss had done good on that, it seemed; the case in my hands would certainly give someone proper motive to kill Burtchell later. The woman he'd put away was a serial killer using both her magical ability and the cover of her status in the nobility to get away with the crimes. Burtchell had caught her red-handed—literally, according to the file—and put her away for a good long while. Or supposedly did. I didn't trust people with these sorts of connections to stay in prison obediently. "Weiss, who's on standby at the prison?"

"Mercado."

Ah, one of the kingsmen I knew. Excellent. "Ask him if Lady Bradshaw is still in."

Penny's head popped up from where she'd been bent over a file at the end of the table. "Cor, I'd nearly forgotten that case! Happened when I was barely in my teens. She'd killed, what was it, eleven people?"

"Thirteen, according to the file. Burtchell was the one who both caught her and put her away."

Weiss gave me an odd look I couldn't decipher. "Lady Bradshaw's sentence, I believe, was fifty years."

I locked eyes with him in challenge. "And powerful, connected people always stay in prison for the full sentence, don't they, Weiss?"

Weiss might have snorted in amusement before he nodded and acquiesced. He withdrew a pad like one of ours and used it with commendable ease.

I set that file aside and grabbed another. Might as well keep looking while we waited on an answer.

"Got one," Penny announced. "Jerry Hatfield, for selling intelligence. Sentenced twenty years, but could be paroled."

Weiss didn't say a word, just picked up his pad again.

We went several hours that way, going through files, listing out suspects. Over half were still in prison. A few had died in the interim. We worked through lunch, none of us willing to come back here unless it was absolutely necessary, and dug our way through the stacks the archivist kept bringing. It was a slow, tedious task, and only the promise of a hot bubble bath later got me through it. Man, I wish this planet had strawberries. I could totally go for chocolate covered strawberries right about now.

Somewhere near quitting time, Sherard put the last file down. "Let's stop here. That gives us four suspects to look into. If none of them pan out, we'll come back."

I stood, stretching, feeling my joints pop and my lower back complain about the hard, wooden chair. As soon as my arms were down, Clint hopped lightly onto my shoulder, using my head for balance as he turned around and got situated. I looked up at him, brow cocked in challenge. "Excuse you. You have four legs, you creature, you can walk yourself."

He gave me a look that said: Now, why would I do that when I have you to carry me?

Someone really needed to explain to me how a magician, who'd never met a cat from Earth and had no idea what they were like, still managed to create its evil twin here in this world. I mean really, parallel universes notwithstanding, what kind of luck did this take?

Weiss didn't say boo to us as we parted at the Archive's door. He turned right, gait still straight, shoulders stiff. We went left, and I breathed properly for the first time in hours. It had been beyond stifling in there with him acting like a disapproving chaperone. Breathing in the outside fresh air also helped to clear the tension out of my system. The air inside the Archives had been stale and musty in the worst sense. Or maybe it just felt that way after a while.

"I mean this in the utmost respect," Penny stated in a tone that said the exact opposite, "but what crawled up his butt and died?"

I laughed. "Well said. Took the words right out of my mouth. Weiss was definitely worse than usual."

Sherard didn't look at all inclined to say something in defense. The words were visibly dragged from his throat. "I actually expected him to be worse. Did you know when we were first informed of Burtchell's murder, he instantly volunteered to investigate?"

Oh man. It made total sense he would do that. Crap, I should have thought of that.

Henri winced. "And the queen instead gave the case to us. That must have gone over well."

"Like rotten fish. I know for a fact, as I was there. She had a good reason for not allowing the request. Weiss and Burtchell were very close friends. He'd have been too emotionally compromised to investigate it properly. That, and the kingsmen are operating at partial strength right now. They really can't afford for Weiss to be off acting detective." Sherard gave a nod to two kingsmen who passed us, both of them familiar, although I didn't know their names. He paused long enough for them to pass out of earshot on the footpath before continuing in a lower voice, "They had quite a row about it that only got worse when I suggested we call you and Henri."

I did a double take and nearly stopped walking. "Wait, it was *your* idea to call me?"

"I think Regina would have thought of it eventually, but it was timing on my part. Weiss was yelling that there wasn't anyone impartial enough to investigate who actually had the skills. I was trying to stop them before they got to the hair-pulling stage. It was almost dog-fight level."

I'd have paid good money to see that. Regina wasn't the type to get physical with people. Then again, how many people were insane enough to get into a physical fight with their queen? "Weiss? Really?!"

"He was…not quite right in that moment. Grief had unhinged him a bit." Sherard grimaced, running a hand through his dark hair before thinking better of it and messing with his perfectly combed do. "It's part of why Regina was adamant about not sending him out. But when he said that, I saw an opening and took it. I suggested sending you. She leapt on the idea. Weiss was fuming but he couldn't argue the point.

She was out the door to go issue the order to you herself before he could get a good rebuttal out."

Now that explained a lot of things. A LOT.

"Well." Henri settled his hat a bit more firmly on his head. "At least that mystery is explained. I'm not sure about the rest of you, but I'm quite famished. If we go now, we might be able to find decent seating at Christopher's."

Steak. Mmmm. "I'm in."

Penny was already nodding in frantic agreement. Sherard gave Henri a nod of approval for a good suggestion. "Lead the way."

It was nice being able to work out of one's own city, although I didn't expect it to last much longer. I had the strangest feeling the answer to this case was in Sheffield. Wasn't quite sure why. Henri, I think, hoped my hunch was wrong, but even he felt it. For all our research and possible suspects yesterday, none of them had felt right.

Still, I enjoyed being in my own space. I got up as usual, dressed in jogging clothes, and went through the routine of making myself a hearty breakfast. I felt like pancakes and fruit this morning. After I ate, I'd take a good jog along my usual route. People were used to seeing a singing, running madwoman by now and no longer tried to stop me or put me in a straitjacket.

From my open window, I heard a bellowed and somewhat panicked, "*CLINT! HELP!*"

My familiar was out the window in a flash, down the fire escape before I could say boo. My own heart leapt into my throat as I snatched up my gun lying on the table, threw open my apartment door, and fled down the stairs, completely reacting on instinct. Henri rarely raised his voice, and I'd not heard that level of distress from him in a while.

Gun in hand, I skidded on the polished wood floor, nearly passing his door in the process, caught my balance, and yanked his door open.

Inside the apartment was sheer chaos.

Clint chased something at high speed, his ears flat against his head as he moved, and boy was he truckin'. He disappeared into Henri's study so fast I saw barely a blur of purple fur and caught no sign of what he chased. The kitchen was in shambles, half the pantry having fallen out, the shelves collapsed, and dry goods and jars spilled out all over the floor, only some of them intact. My friend was crouched on the island like a damsel in distress, liberally covered in white flour around his head and shoulders.

It was so comical my adrenaline died down and I felt a little foolish for arriving with gun in hand. "Henri, what on earth—"

Still crouched on the island, he said plaintively, "There's a rat in here! A *huge* rat. Sodding deities, I didn't know they could get that big."

A rat. Caused this mess? "Start at the beginning."

He flung out a hand to stop me. A wand was in his other, and he used it to point towards the floor in illustration. "Wait, don't come in here if you don't have shoes on. At least three jars broke."

I lifted a foot so he could see I had my tennis shoes on. "I'm good. What happened?"

"I was cooking, and when I went to fetch something from the pantry, this huge creature was on the top shelf, digging into my sugar." Henri reported as if it was a personal affront and he'd take it to the highest authority.

He was still in robes and PJ's, a clear indication he'd been caught very unawares by this rodent invader. It was rare to see him in this state of dishabille, as he was normally in suits and all buttoned up. For some reason, he looked very pokeable. I had to restrain the urge to go over and muss him up some more.

"I hit it with a spell but the dastardly thing escaped. And

it collapsed three shelves in the process."

More like, he panicked, used a spell he probably shouldn't have, and that collapsed three shelves. I found it hysterical my friend could calmly face down criminals and rogue magicians without flinching, but find a rat in his beloved pantry and he went pear-shaped. "Well, Clint will get it for you."

"I've never been so glad I acquired him for you. He's truly a useful creature to have." Henri looked down at the mess on his floor with a grimace and lamented, "I was going to have pancakes."

Can't laugh, can't laugh, can't laugh…. "How about this. I'll help you clean up, and then you can come up to my place, okay? I was making pancakes myself."

He perked up slightly. "The fluffy ones you make?"

"Absolutely. You got a cleaning spell in your arsenal?" I ignored the Tom and Jerry chase zooming around the apartment. Clint would get him. Although man, I could see why Henri freaked out. That rat was the size of a small cat. *I'd* freak out and likely shoot it.

There was a high-pitched, animalistic scream of pain, and then silence from Henri's study. Clint sauntered out with the rat in its mouth, like a prize fighter would a trophy. He dropped it in the center of the room and groomed his mouth and paw in a smug way.

"Clint, you are the best Felix ever." Henri finally uncurled from his perch, regarding the rat with distaste. "I should have just called for you from the beginning."

I very carefully did not agree. Oh, the tempting things we leave unsaid in the wrong moments. Or right ones. "Come on, boys, let's clean up."

Henri, perhaps you should get a Felix next...you know, in case of any more mice.

It was a RAT, Seaton, and it was half Clint's size!
  Tell him, Janie.

Tell him I found you standing on top of your kitchen island,

 surrounded by glass and covered in flour?

  I'm never going to live this down, am I?
      NOPE   NOPE

Report 16: Dead-ends

Jamie was still chuckling over the whole rat debacle as we headed into the station an hour later. I did not find it in the least amusing to be ambushed by a rodent in my own pantry. As we headed in, I shot her a scathing look. "Stop snickering."

Of course, that made her snicker all the more loudly, drawing more than a few curious looks from our colleagues in the hall.

"If *you* encountered a rodent of unusual size in your pantry, you'd not be so entertained," I growled at her, although I kept my tone low in an effort to not have this business all over the station.

For some reason, she threw her head back and laughed louder. "It's an ROUS!"

"A what?" Sometimes I did not understand her reactions. Actually, most of the time that was the case.

"*Princess Bride.* Remind me, I'll tell you the story later."

I felt only slightly mollified by this promise. I did enjoy her stories from Earth.

"Wait, if that was an ROUS—does that make you Buttercup?" Mirth rolled from her at this notion, whatever it was. "Oooh, wait, does that make me Wesley? Gender role switch!"

"Now what is she prattling on about?" Seaton demanded of us. He was leaning against Jamie's desk, texting pad in his hands, looking quite peeved.

I felt like I should corner the market on being peeved this morning, but it was a petty feeling. I strove to be more civilized. "Good morning, Seaton. She's laughing at my misfortune. I had an unfortunate encounter with a large rat in my pantry while making breakfast."

"Yours isn't the only unfortunate encounter," Seaton informed me. "Although at least yours could be handily dealt with. I can't kill mine."

"That doesn't sound ominous or anything." Jamie slung her bag into her chair, her humor finally dying down. "What bit you?"

"Weiss." Seaton made an aggrieved sound low in his throat, much akin to a wolf denied prey. "That lovely list of suspects we created? He carried on the investigation after we broke off for the day. He ran me down this morning before I could even leave my house and informed me they were all dead ends. Everyone had a staunch alibi for their whereabouts the day of Burtchell's murder. He also informed me if I didn't start taking this case seriously, he'd take us all off the case."

"Tosser," I summarized unhappily. "Wait, does he have the authority to do that?"

"Not in the slightest. We're equal in rank."

"I thought so. Well, at least he's saved us some legwork. Although that means we're once again back to the drawing board."

Jamie also made a face, dropping into her chair and scooting her bag unceremoniously to the side. "There's that. And frankly, I don't feel like we're barking up the right tree anyway. All those people we looked into yesterday had the motive, but few of them had the means. And apparently none of them the opportunity. We established there was enough foot traffic along Burtchell's street that morning that if a stranger was nearby, someone would have spotted them."

"You think we're looking at a native." I couldn't fault her logic. Except for one minor detail. "But most of the natives adored him."

"Not necessarily a native," she corrected me. "But someone who had every right to be in town. Who the townspeople saw often. Or at least someone who was of the right profession to have a reason to be there. That list you guys gave me before, of the different type of magicians who could do the wind spell. Wouldn't those same professionals have a sort of incognito appearance in Sheffield? I mean, no one would really remark on them being there."

Seaton and I exchanged a look. The royal mage lifted his shoulders in an elegant shrug. "She rather does have a point, old chap."

"Well, yes, but we went this route for a reason. Going through every single windwhisperer, hedge wizard, and crafter in the greater Sheffield area is going to be tedious in the extreme. Not to mention time-consuming. Finding someone with a potential motive first is faster." Not to mention it would involve a great deal of driving. I valued living. I'd really rather not give Jamie multiple reasons to assume the wheel.

McSparrin appeared from somewhere to join us. "What's happened?"

Seaton succinctly summarized Weiss's actions, and McSparrin's open face clouded darkly. "That was awfully nice of him."

"Stepping on toes, that one." Seaton shook his head. "I can understand his persistence—it was his friend killed. But at the same time, he's a seasoned agent. He should know how to pace himself during an investigation."

I thought of how I might feel and react if Jamie was the one murdered. I did not think I'd operate with the cool head Seaton expected. In fact, I was rather sure I'd be reacting stronger than Weiss was now. I shook the depressing thought off, concentrating more on the matter at hand. "McSparrin, to catch you up, Jamie believes that we're hunting in the wrong pack anyway. She believes our murderer is closer to Sheffield, someone who goes through the town often enough no one would remark on his or her presence."

"I did think of that too," McSparrin admitted. "I started going back through the letters this morning, and I know we ruled a lot of them out, but a few were downright disturbing. And anonymous. Burtchell bore a lot of hate from people who thought he should have done more."

"But they were all anonymous, right? Hard to track those people down."

Jamie shook her head at Seaton. "No, that's precisely my point. I think someone more local to Burtchell is behind this. If they took the effort to stay anonymous, then it means they knew it could be traced back to them. I was hoping for a quick and easy suspect list, hence why we went through the archives. Well, that, and because we needed to make sure none of these people had anything to do with it. This murder speaks of cold calculation but also a lot of rage. Killing a person point blank like that takes a lot of emotion to pull off. And rage like that is hard to sustain. Any emotion is, if you think about it. The emotional highs are easy to feel, but they usually simmer down to something manageable. The mind regulates emotion so you don't go crazy with it. And given enough time, most people talk themselves out of rash and stupid decisions like murder."

"Murders either happen in the heat of the moment or because the emotion is so strong it sticks with a person," McSparrin agreed. "I remember you saying that. You think in this case, the rage was hot?"

"Hot enough, at least. It makes me think those letters might be the motive. Even if they won't lead us to a suspect directly."

"I can't fault the logic," I admitted freely.

Seaton nodded in agreement. "And I can't think of any other leads to follow. But the letters are by and large useless. You aren't really suggesting looking up every hedge witch, crafter, and windwhisperer in that area and investigating them, are you?"

Jamie looked about at all our faces. "Anyone else got a better idea?"

Silence.

My shoulders slumped in resignation. "This is going to take a while."

We didn't see anything else for it and packed up. At least this time we'd be traveling in the relative coolness of the morning. Seaton, bless his everlasting soul, drove. Jamie seemed both resigned and impatient at the pace. I'd heard her rant about "speed isn't dangerous" too many times to invite a repetition and chose to let it ride.

But this time while we were on the very long, windy road towards Sheffield, at least one person had thought to plan ahead. Jamie pulled out several sheets of paper she called Mad-Libs and proceeded to teach us the game. The random words we supplied her made the bland story absolutely ridiculous and we laughed most of the trip in.

This was, yet again, something else she could introduce into our society and make a pretty penny off it. I sometimes questioned why she so insisted on being a detective. She could spend her days inventing things and never run out of either ideas or money. I did wonder what it was about her nature that so compelled her to solve crimes.

Not that I was complaining. Far from it. I'd never have met her through normal circles. And the idea of spending the rest of my career locked up in my lab, doing both my work and Sanderson's, was strangely cold. I'd not known I needed a partner until fate handed me one. Well, fate and Gregson.

When the Mad-Libs game grew to be tiring, we buckled down into work and split up Burtchell's finances. With three sets of eyes, it was easy to check over everything he'd done in the past three years, which was all we were interested in. Nothing stood out to me and neither woman found anything of interest to note.

We got in to Sheffield at roughly noon, checking into the same hotel as before. It took us only minutes to put our bags into our respective rooms, then we went back down to the dining room for lunch. It was the right time for it, after all, and it wasn't like we had a firm plan of how to move forward.

Everyone ordered and sat back, enjoying the relative coolness of the dining room. I turned my mind to the problem of finding a suspect we knew barely anything about and frowned as a solution failed to leap out at me.

"A census would tell us all the magicians in this area," McSparrin noted, clearly thinking along the same lines. She loosened the top two buttons of her uniform as she spoke, a silent concession to the heat. "But I don't know how helpful that would be."

"Fairly helpful. It'll give us a starting point, at least." Seaton tapped his fingers against the tabletop, lips pursed. "I'm inclined to ask the constables about the letters as well. Surely Burtchell reported them? And if nothing else, perhaps they can supply us with a few names of people who were publicly calling for Burtchell's head."

Jamie nodded in support. "Let's do both, see if there's any overlap. Henri and I will take the constables, you two go look up the census."

"Start in Sheffield, work our way out?" I asked.

"Only sensible approach." A ripple of emotion crossed her face, and she spoke slowly, each word paving the way forward. "I think we should look up the ship rosters as well. Cross-check them with the protesters. Either someone wanted revenge for a life lost, or perhaps one of the survivors from the wreck is getting revenge themselves."

I foresaw a great many lists in our future. "You're quite sure the ships are somehow involved, aren't you?"

"Call it a hunch. It was the only recent thing people were mad at Burtchell for. If it's not that, I honestly don't know what else to look at. His finances were relatively clean."

Burtchell was the rare gambler who had a budget for his vice and stuck to it. He was financially sound and I saw nothing in them indicating trouble. I didn't see any IOUs where people owed him money, either. It was yet another dead end.

This case would drive us insane soon if we didn't wrest a lead from somewhere.

"Whoever did this is too clever by half," McSparrin lamented before picking up her glass and taking a healthy swallow of the iced beverage. "Normally we have at least some idea, or a witness who saw something strange. It's like he's invisible."

"Or just the sort of man you wouldn't notice." Jamie said with a nostalgic tone. Whatever it was she recalled, she didn't choose to share. "Well! Let's hope this time we get a suspect that sticks."

I seconded that whole-heartedly.

We ate, not quite at our leisure, but without any true rush. As we left the hotel, each going their own way, Jamie left the motorcar to Seaton and McSparrin. I was prayerfully thankful for her generosity, even if it meant we walked in the increasingly warm summer day.

We'd barely crossed the street when she broached the subject I'd meant to discuss with her. "Did Gregson tell you the kingsmen want us for consultants?"

"He did, yesterday afternoon. I'd not found a good time to talk with you about this. What did you think of the offer?"

"I'm a little surprised, honestly. I mean, you've seen how Weiss reacts to me."

My nose wrinkled up in distaste. "Yes, quite. I think in this case he's been overruled by both Queen Regina and Seaton."

"That's my take on it." Her eyes scrutinized me, a query open on her face. "Are you for or against this idea?"

"I'm open to it. But Jamie, if it means working under a superior who so openly dislikes you, I'm not inclined to accept it. Such situations are not just uncomfortable, but potentially dangerous. What if he ignores a call for backup? What if he gives you a case that's dangerous just because he wants to safeguard his own people? He might be the type to think of people as expendable."

She didn't discount my fears. Her stride steady, she walked at my pace, and mulled for a time. "I think if we do this, we'll need to stipulate that Seaton's my supervisor. Or he has to sign off on any assignment I take. I mean, really, my core is unstable enough that he should be alerted to where I am anyway."

"An excellent point." It was also a sound plan. Seaton would agree to such a term in a heartbeat. "So you truly wish to do this, then?"

"I was hesitant to take any sort of consulting position with the kingsmen because I'm not literate and don't know the culture. I've got a better grasp on both at this point, so I won't be a fish out of water. Well, not as much as I was. But you'll be with me," she added with heartfelt simplicity. "There's not much I can't do without you."

Those words, that sentiment, hit me with the force

of a spell right in my chest. It was empowering and humbling all at once. I wanted to wrap her up in an embrace tight enough to make bones squeak in protest.

Perhaps this showed on my face. More likely she shared at least part of the same impulse, as she wrapped an arm around my shoulders and hugged me tight to her side for a moment. It threw off my balance and stride and I didn't care a whit. I leaned into her, and indulged for a moment. It wasn't exactly appropriate, and I didn't care. For once, I wished for propriety to go hang itself.

It was over in seconds, leaving me feeling oddly bereft. A bright smile graced her face and there was a noticeable bounce in her stride. "Are we doing this, then?"

"Yes. Assuming they agree to our conditions." I must be mad. Why was I agreeing to yet even more work?

I blamed her for this.

Awww, Henri. I can hug you more often, you know. I love hugs.

It's not appropriate for a woman to hug another man.

Is that a no?

Since when did you care about propriety? Do as you wish.

-cackles-

Report 17: Finally, a Lead!

There were far too many lists of names for my peace of mind. Henri and I had some, Sherard and Penny had another, and there was the stack of letters to go through. I expected the truly troublesome ones to be anonymous, but you know what they say about assumptions...better to cross-check them. Anyone who was either a magician themselves or had intimate ties with a magician went on the chalkboard.

The hotel, bless them, had readily given the small conference room back to us to work out of. Constable Parmenter had joined us, apparently talked into doing so by Penny. Having one local in the group to help sort out people would save a lot of time.

Parmenter was patient in this process the first hour, calling out names along with the rest. We were all around the table, me slouching, Clint lounging on the table's surface nearby and dozing. Penny manned the chalkboard, which left the men to handle the various lists and call out names. It was a tedious, tedious process and more than once I wished for a computer. A good database would have sorted this all by now and given us a list to start from.

"I'm sorry, I'm not clear on this," Parmenter stated. His pointed ears lay flat against his head. He'd been fidgety and confused for the past hour so it was no surprise he objected. More of a surprise it had taken him this long to voice it. "I thought it would take a powerful magician to get through a royal mage's wards."

"Technically, you're right," Sherard explained absently. "But in this case, the wards never failed. They were bypassed entirely. Amelia Johnson."

Penny dutifully wrote it down.

Seeing Sherard lose the thread, I picked up the explanation for Parmenter's sake. "You see, our murderer was clever enough to slip in when the wards were off. He waited while Burtchell was talking with his friend, slipped in through the front door in between the morning deliveries, then waited upstairs until everyone was gone. Went down, killed Burtchell, then went upstairs again. When the housekeeper came, she left both doors open and unlocked as she ran for help. All he had to do was walk out."

Parmenter stared at me incredulously. "You know that for a fact?"

"No, but it's the only thing that makes sense. Even now the wards are still up and functional. If someone had battered through them in order to get inside or out, we'd see damage. They wouldn't be humming merrily along. And the only place no one occupied at all that morning was upstairs. It was the perfect place to hide."

"It's also why we're fairly sure the murderer either lives or works in this area," Penny added. "Any stranger would have been remarked upon. He was able to walk about without gathering notice. It has to be a familiar face."

"Familiar enough that he could watch RM Burtchell's house long enough to get his patterns down, too," Parmenter said slowly, the pieces visibly falling into place for him. "Cor mighty, makes more sense now why you're doing all this. This person, would they need to be physically strong? Fast, or dexterous?"

I shook my head. "No. It didn't take any of that in order to perform the murder. I wish we could narrow the suspects that way, but unfortunately the only thing we're sure of is that they had very good control of wind spells. That, and they were enraged enough to ambush a royal mage in his own home."

Parmenter frowned at the stack of letters in Sherard's hands. "And you're including them because you think someone was mad enough about the sunken ships to kill him? That's your motive?"

Henri cast him a glance over the papers in his hands. "Possibly. It's the only thing recent. Every other case Burtchell was on that ended with either death or incarceration is years old. And those people all had alibis."

"That's what you went into Kingston to check." Parmenter grunted in understanding. "Still. I know some people were upset RM Burtchell didn't save every ship—and one of them lost almost the entire crew—but Burtchell was only one man. None of us really blamed him for it."

My ears perked. "Wait, this is the first I've heard one of the ship's crews was lost. I thought the ships themselves were lost, but the people largely saved?"

Parmenter shook his head and corrected, "Three of the ships were saved intact, vessel and passengers both. Two of the ships were larger trading vessels. I was standing near RM Burtchell when we called him to help. It was a bad storm, miss. Ah, Detective. Powerful bad. Not seen a storm like that one in fifty years. I could barely see my nose on my face, and RM Burtchell had to light up the area with all sorts of spells just to get some visibility. He told me outright he couldn't save all five. Said even in the height of his power, he couldn't do that. And the two trading vessels were powerful large, both six masts and a good seven hundred feet sparred."

I had to translate that last bit. I believed he meant the hull alone was seven hundred feet. And if that was correct, then that was a stupidly massive ship. You couldn't get much bigger than that and keep something afloat and steerable. Not for a wooden sailing ship. I let out a low whistle.

He gave me a nod, agreeing with the unvoiced sentiment. "I didn't blame him for the decision. Only sensible one to be made. If he tried for all five, he'd have lost all five. He went for the three smaller ones first, as they were passenger ships, and closest. Got them lifted out of the sea intact and set them at the docks. By the time he could react to the trading ships, one of them was already dashed onto the rocks, and there was no helping it. The other he held steady until we could get rowing boats out there, try to get the crew off at least. The ship was a loss—it and the cargo went down after he released his magic. Lost three hundred and sixty-two souls that night. But he saved over fifteen hundred."

"Someone thinks he should have saved all two thousand," I noted with a sigh. "Or at least, a different fifteen hundred."

Parmenter hesitated a long moment, eyeing the lists and letters with a perturbed look on his face.

"Out with it, man." Sherard poked him with the eraser end of a pencil.

"It's just…there were two windwhisperers on the trading vessels." Parmenter worried on the end of his once immaculate mustache. I recognized a nervous tic when I saw it. "One of them's laid up, now, had two broken legs as a souvenir. He's resting up in the next town over, I think, with his folks. The other was a survivor of the ship that lost the entire crew."

I shared a glance with the other three. That sounded like a good possibility.

"He's not going to be on your lists," Parmenter added, frown deepening. "Martin…was his name, I think. He was powerful upset about what happened, I had to throw him in the drunk tank one night. Got six sheets to the wind and raving about how wrong the whole situation was and everyone involved was a—" He cut himself off, glancing between me and Penny. "Well, you can no doubt guess what he said. He was angry enough to start random fights with people, although I'd thought I'd talked him out of it. We went into all that happened, how Burtchell couldn't save them all. How all the rescuers on scene had done everything they could. I thought he'd seen reason."

"Anger and grief normally don't." I knew that from painful and personal experience. "Why do you say he won't be on the lists? He's not from here?"

"No, Detective, he was just here temporarily until his company got him on a new ship. Stayed in the boarding house here a while. Not sure when he left, only I stopped seeing him in the pub…" Parmenter trailed off and buried his head in one hand. He looked ruddy from either embarrassment or some other emotion. "Blight the bastard. You think he did it?"

"I think he's a good candidate. What's the shipping company he works for?"

"Reed and Bell."

I was all for abandoning the lists. This sounded like a much better lead to follow through on. "Let's look him up, see if we can't have a chat. Even if it isn't our man, he might well know someone else for us to talk to."

Reed and Bell was a large enough company to have a building, warehouse, and a set of docks all for their private use. The reason why I know this? Because it took several phone calls to find the right number for their office. For all they were listed in the directory, the numbers weren't in the right order, and my first try for the office instead got me the dock foreman.

Standing in the hotel lobby with the receiver cradled between my ear and shoulder, I went through the numbers. Each person I tried wasn't sure who could answer my question, which left me trying someone else. I felt the keen stare of people passing me by. I tried to keep my voice down, but the mic sensitivity on these phones was crap. I had to half-yell and keep each word distinct. Whoever invented these things, it wasn't Graham Bell. Maybe I needed to sic Ellie on this problem.

Finally, I got the right woman on the phone. Or at least, the head office. "Hello. I'm Detective Jamie Edwards with the Kingston PD. I need to speak with someone who'd know your employee roster."

"*Yes, Detective, I can help you with that.*"

Thank all the saints. "Excellent. I'm looking for Robert

Martin."

"*Oh, my,*" a raspy alto voice answered, sounding both alarmed and ready for some juicy gossip. Ah. THAT type. "*Dear me, has Mr. Martin done something?*"

"More like, I think he witnessed something." I wasn't about to air it around that I wanted him for a murder suspect. The man would disappear completely even if he hadn't done anything. People spooked easily when the police came knocking. "Can you tell me where to find him?"

"*Yes, one moment, Detective.*" I heard the sound of some file cabinets opening and closing, paper rustling, all of it muted and distorted with the scratchy, underwater sound of the lines. I winced and kept the receiver a good three inches from my ear. Seriously, Ellie and I were having a talk after this case was done. The phone made a clack as the woman picked it up again. "*According to the schedule, he's on the* Windsprite. *He's due back in to Kingston port in two days.*"

Two days, huh? That gave us a day to follow up on leads here, see if anything panned out. "Afternoon or morning?"

"*Oh, I'd think afternoon at earliest. They're coming from* Wind Capers."

I had a vague idea where that was. At some point, I really needed to sit down and study the geography, get it memorized. "Thank you very much for the help."

With great relief, I hung up and massaged my aching ear. Owww. But at least the pain was worth it. Or would be, if this was the right guy. I went back into the conference room, taking a look at the chalkboard as I moved. A few more names on the list had been added while I was yelling into a phone. We were up to four people now.

Penny looked round as I came in and asked hopefully, "You found him?"

"I did. He's on a ship at the moment, and due back into Kingston in two days, probably the afternoon. I made it sound like he was a witness to something. Let's not spook him."

"Or spread potentially damaging rumors," Henri added, still focused on the list in front of him. "All he's really guilty of, that we know of, is getting drunk and disorderly at a pub. It could be he's not our man."

Trust it to Henri to point that out. He's always very considerate of other people. Even potential suspects. "There's that, too."

"Two days," Sherard repeated, tossing his list down. Clint immediately pounced on it, arranging the loose sheets of paper like a magpie building a nest. The mage frowned down at the Felix. "Clint, you may not have those."

Clint stopped, paw still on paper, and flattened his ears in a pitiful manner. "No?"

Sherard sighed, relenting. Softy. "Not yet, anyway. After I'm done."

Yeah, that was not nearly firm enough to make headway. I picked up my cat before he could dig his claws in. He came happily, rubbing up against my chin and purring as I gave him a good scratch on his chest. It was the only surefire technique to derailing his magpie tendencies.

"Two days to track down and question potential suspects before we need to drive back into Kingston. I figure, alert someone at the station to go the docks and pick him up, just in case we're late getting in."

Penny nodded and volunteered, "I can call it in. Captain Gregson likely wants an update anyway."

Better her ears than mine. "Sure. Urk, wait, that means I'm once again updating the queen."

They all gave me these big, cheesy, false grins. Some friends I had.

"I don't wanna," I whined and rolled my eyes beseechingly at Henri. "Isn't it your turn?"

As expected, he caved. "Oh, very well, I suppose I can do it once more on your behalf. But may I remind you, it's *you* she requested on this case."

I gave him a winsome smile. "It's okay, Henri, she likes you too."

His dark eyes gave me that flat look. We both knew that had nothing to do with anything. But, being a true gentleman

and friend, he was willing to take one for the team.
There's a reason Henri's my favorite.

Wait a minute, I thought I was your favorite!

You were. Then you deserted me. Henri's my favorite now.

You're only saying that because he gives you chocolate.

'xcuse you very much, I do not! She steals my chocola
that is entirely a different thing altogether.

Give, steal, what's the difference?

Says the police detective.

Report 18: A Break in the Case

Lots of things break, anyway.

Too true.

In the end, only about seven viable people had the right expertise to be possible suspects. The first two we spoke with were injured, and injured badly enough I didn't see how they could sneak anywhere. Jamie agreed with me so those interviews were brief in nature. The third woman on our list had moved some months ago and was up on the northern coast now. No one had seen her since the move. Likely not our suspect.

Seaton and McSparrin had taken the other four, and that left us with only one other person to interview: the boardinghouse owner where Robert Martin, the windwhisperer, had stayed while here in Sheffield.

After all, we needed to establish how long he'd stayed in Sheffield. If the timeline didn't fit, there was no reason to track the man down.

Abigail's Boardinghouse was a neatly kept house that bordered on being a hotel. It had to be a hundred rooms at least, and the white clapboard sprawled along the street. I saw occupations of all types sitting around the wide front porch, everything from traveling salesmen to sailors. Miss Abigail apparently maintained a thriving business here.

Jamie strode right up the stairs and toward the front door. One of the men moved to intercept her, an arm barring her way, although he doffed his hat and gave her a deferential nod of the head. Body language made it clear he wasn't looking for a fight. "Miss. This is a bachelor's-only boardinghouse."

My partner flicked her coat aside to show the badge on her belt. "Detective, actually, and I'm not staying. I need to ask the owner a few questions. Do you know where she is?"

His attitude did an about-turn. "Oh. Certainly, Detective. She's out back, likely, tending to her garden."

"Thank you." Jamie gave him a polite smile and we both turned to walk along the porch, heading for the side of the house. We garnered more than a few curious looks as we passed the men, but no one else seemed inclined to stop and ask questions.

The back of the boardinghouse wasn't quite as I expected. Every square inch of the yard was filled with plants, mostly of the edible variety. Miss Abigail apparently supplemented her table with her own vegetables, which was both frugal and smart when feeding this many mouths. It was lovingly tended by the woman in the wide-brimmed straw hat. She heard our approach and turned her head, wiping off her hands with the apron around her waist as she gained her feet.

"Hello," Jamie greeted in a friendly way. "I'm Detective Edwards. This is my partner, Dr. Davenforth. Can we have a minute? I need to ask a few questions about one of your former boarders."

The matron looked worried, as many people did when a policeman came calling unannounced. "Well, that's fine, but I likely can't tell you much. I keep track of when they come and when they go, but that's all. They're free to do as they please as long as they abide by the rules."

"It's the coming and going that we need an answer to," she assured the woman. "Robert Martin."

I could tell the name rang a bell for her but Abigail wasn't entirely sure who we meant. It was a rather common name. I tacked on helpfully, "Windwhisperer? One of the survivors from the sunk trading ships?"

Before I could trot it all out, her eyes lit up in recognition. "Oh, sure, him. Now that was a sad case, that was. They had me take in anyone from the crews, as well as some of the stranded passengers. I was glad to help, but it was such a sorry business all around. People injured, and shaken, and some of them crying these silent tears. More than a few lost friends and loved ones, others were destitute, as most of what they owned went down to the ocean floor. We all pitched in and helped as we could, of course. The two survivors from that ship you mentioned, they took it the hardest. Drank more than a bit, and we let them, as sometimes a man needs to drown his sorrows. Mr. Martin, he especially took it terrible bad. Kept saying over and over that the royal mage should have done more than that, and why hadn't he saved everyone. Grief does that, you know."

"Yes, it was a sad business all around," I said noncommittally. "Mr. Martin stayed with you for a few days, then?"

"Oh, it was longer than that. He didn't stay in the house most of the day. Only for breakfast and to sleep, far as I could tell. I'm not sure where he was during the day but he always came in smelling of beer, so..." Abigail trailed off with a knowing look. "One can guess. His company had him stay put until he could be reassigned to another ship, he said. What with the wreckage to sort out, and insurance investigations, and all that, I suppose it would take time. He was here almost two weeks."

Alarm bells rang. Why would the company force him to stay here for two weeks? Why not let him go home and recuperate? Even if he had no real family to speak of, surely he had his own place. Why stay here, when he had neither kith nor kin? I shot Jamie a glance and saw the same questions scrawled on her face, masked by a carefully neutral expression.

"Do you remember what day he left?"

"Same day RM Burtchell died." Abigail's countenance fell a mite. "He came in, smiling ear to ear, and said he'd been contacted by his company and had a new berth. He'd barely packed and gotten his ticket when the news hit that RM Burtchell had been murdered. He didn't seem to care, really; he was still smiling. I understand how a man likes to have work, I do, but the rest of us were in such a state...I barely got anything done the rest of the day, I was so rattled by the news."

It did sound disturbing, his reaction. I counselled myself to not jump to conclusions. Being happy at someone's demise was not the same as participating in their murder. Take Sanderson, for instance. I'd be thrilled if someone removed him from the world even though I wouldn't stoop to murdering him.

"Thank you, Miss Abigail, that's all we have at the moment. I just wanted to check his whereabouts." Jamie gave another one of those disarming smiles that seemed to come so naturally to her. It put the woman at ease, as she likely intended it to do. "We might need to come back if we think of something further."

"Oh, certainly, that's fine. I'm always here."

We said goodbyes and walked out. I waited until we were far from the boardinghouse before voicing the words we were both thinking. "That timing and reaction don't look good for Robert Martin."

"Not in the least." Jamie shot me a wide smile, practically bouncing. "Finally, we have a lead. It's about time we got a break in this case."

"Hear, hear." I cast a glance towards the sky and frowned thoughtfully, logistics running through my mind. "It's a bit too late in the evening to consider driving back to Kingston."

"Yeah, and we need to follow up with the other two, see if they struck anything likely. If they did, we need to follow up on it tomorrow. If not, maybe leave in the morning?"

"Might as well."

All of the people on Seaton's and McSparrin's list had alibis. That rather ended all of our potential leads in Sheffield. I hoped and prayed that meant our remaining lead was solid and would actually give us the killer. If it wasn't Martin, I truly didn't know where else to go from here.

We packed up the next morning and drove in. Jamie, somehow, wrested the keys from us and had the car going thirty-five the entire way back. I was at first anxious about her speed, but the car stayed true and steady on the road, and after thirty minutes of nothing happening but the sea breeze ruffling my hair, I slowly relaxed. It was a quieter trip than the previous ones, but I think it was mostly due to exhaustion. We were all heartily sick of this drive.

By the time we did make it in, there wasn't much to be done, as our suspect wouldn't be in until tomorrow afternoon. Jamie drove us straight to the precinct, where we split ways. She went in to speak with Gregson and give him a verbal update of where we stood at the moment. I lingered in order to put my equipment back up. I hadn't used any of it on this last trip to Sheffield, so there was nothing to tidy or write a report on. Just a matter of putting things back in their proper places on my lab's shelves.

With my back to the door, I didn't think much of the sound of the hinges moving, nor the quick march of footsteps coming inside. I'd been gone several days, after all, surely a colleague had a question for me. Or even had noticed my presence and stopped in to offer a simple hello. Police stations thrived on gossip; perhaps this person wanted an update on our bizarre case. I turned with a pleasant greeting on the tip of my tongue.

Instinct sent me down, dropping like a puppet with its strings cut, as a sizzle of magical fire flew over my head. Sodding deities, what in blazes?!

The jars of specimens and chemicals over my head burst as the flames hit them, and I yelped, rolling frantically out of the way before I was hit by something. I could hear and see the fire suppressant hexes around my lab walls engage, smothering the flames before they could spread, but it did no good. Another attack followed the first within seconds. This time, I heard the casting spell.

"*Infercino!*" Sanderson screamed out.

Even as I yanked my wand out of my interior breast pocket, I snapped out, "Sanderson! HAVE YOU TAKEN LEAVE OF WHAT'S LEFT OF YOUR SENSES! Cease and desist at once!"

"I hate you, you brownnosing little prick," Sanderson snarled from somewhere over…there. He wasn't in front of the door anymore, he was moving around the table. "You've gotten me suspended, likely fired, and for what!"

I threw up the strongest shielding spell I knew, then did it again, doubling it in layers. He'd either gone mad and was here for revenge, or he had let anger get the better of his judgement, as usual. It could be either, or both, but I really didn't care much what his motives were. I just needed to get free of this room. It was a death trap, with only the one door in and out. How long until someone heard him, realized something was wrong? I was in the back right wing of the new building for a reason. It was remote enough that if something magically went awry, it wouldn't impact the whole station. As logical as that was, it might doom me in this moment.

I moved as stealthily as I could to the right, trying to keep the table between us. My worktable had its

Magic Outside the Box   185

own protections carved into the base of the top, and it offered a considerable amount of protection. If I could utilize it. "Sanderson, be sensible. I'm only a magical examiner. My word—"

"Oh, don't play that card with me," he sneered and threw off another spell that singed along the top of my shields this time. It bounced off, but it was a brutal shock. He'd used a stone-crushing spell that time, and the impact made me slide back three inches on the polished wood floors. "You got Seaton to do it. You're all chummy with him now, of course he'd be willing to do you a little favor. You're a benighted coward, Davenforth! Face me!"

The paperwork involved when someone on the force was hurt was best described as *tomes*. And that's in the case of an accident or an injury sustained during the course of duty. I didn't want to fathom what it would be on purpose. As tempting as it was to pop Sanderson one, did I want to be stuck writing an incident report about the imbecile for the next decade? Hardly.

Even with all this screaming and magic being thrown about, no help came. Fine. I could organize my own rescue when needed. I jerked my texting pad free of my pocket, toggling both Jamie and Seaton as the recipients, and wrote in a quick scrawl: *SOS*. They'd both know what the cryptic message meant.

Then I decided enough was enough. Sanderson wanted me to poke my head up, likely so he could whack it right off my shoulders. No, thank you. But it was best to play along with idiots to some degree. I snagged my stool and threw it up in the air. Sure enough, as soon as it cleared the table, he blasted it apart with another stone-crushing spell. Repetitive, wasn't he?

I barely gave the splinters time to fly before I popped up as well, this time with my own spell at the ready. I threw the Hunter's Trap at him, but I wasn't the only one with shields up. The magical net bounced off, entangling around one of my microscopes instead. I ducked down again with a curse. Untangling the microscope was going to be tedious in the extreme. *Curse* Sanderson.

My eyes searched the shelves behind Sanderson frantically, trying to find something to use. His shields only protected his front and sides, not behind or above him. Typical of its type, and easy to exploit if one knew how. Of course, I knew how, as it was my business to. He wasn't employing that weakness against me, likely because I had nothing but a wall of files behind me. Aside from toppling the bookcase, there was nothing else he could do with it. Well, come to think of it, that would hurt.

I scanned the shelves behind him. Books, jars of sea tears, collection of hexes...no, no, no, all wrong, nothing helpful—wait. Captured spectral energy from mine and Jamie's first case together. I caught it with a flick of my wand, yanking its lid off and sharply down. The energy splattered against the top of his head in a well-aimed arc, splattering against his shields and disintegrating them like sugar in boiling water. He yelped in surprise, then snarled like a wounded bear, his rage loud and echoing in the small room.

I saw my chance to gain the door and stood, shield still at max readiness, ready to either fling a spell at him or dive for cover. For the first time, I saw his face, and he looked mad. Utterly mad, no rationality in his expression.

It arrested me for a second, my body frozen. What had pushed him so completely over the edge? Even if he were facing unemployment, it was just a job, wasn't it? Surely this wasn't the end of the line for him. He was still a licensed mage, after all.

He lifted his wand with a deliberateness that spoke of trouble. I saw his magic building, his mouth forming the words to a spell no human being should ever use against another. The blood in my veins turned to ice. My shields wouldn't protect me from that. Not even a sturdy wall of brick, which was behind me, would stop that spell. What could I do?

My mind raced through possibilities even as my instincts urged me to run, to find cover. The two were at war with each other. Dread seized me before I could make any snap decisions because the truth was, I couldn't move fast enough to evade him. Evading a spell was like evading a bullet—what human being had the reflexes to do that? I was a dead man and a shriek of helpless rage caterwauled through my mind, echoing and ravaging, as I stared death in the face.

The cock of a hammer pin being pulled into place sounded thunderously loud in the relative silence. A hand I knew well rested on my back, and I could sense her, even though she was still a half-step behind me.

The Shinigami had arrived.

Even Sanderson paused and he stared at her with hatred but also fear, his mouth working without making a sound, the wand in his hand wavering as it pointed at me.

"Sanderson, dismiss the spell." Jamie Edwards did not make the request. The God of Death she was named after spoke, and her words were utterly final.

Sanderson quivered in place. I was prepared to throw us both to the ground, nearly vibrating, my nerves were so tightly sprung. The spectral energy was splashed all over the other side of the room, around Sanderson, and I could not afford for Jamie to get anywhere near it. She seemed to be intent on staying next to me, though, thankfully. Multiple footsteps raced down the corridor. I heard Gregson calling out questions as he came.

Neither of us looked around or tried to answer him. It was a death sentence if we broke this tableau—we all knew that. Sanderson stared at her hard, wand still shaking, the white of his eyes clear. He was terrified now. Whatever expression Jamie wore must have been ferocious in the extreme. Nerves jittered under my skin, adrenaline racing. I didn't know what he'd do next. I absolutely couldn't let either myself or Jamie become victims to his fit of madness.

"You'd shoot me, wouldn't you? Just to save him?"

Jamie let out a scoffing laugh ringing with echoes of the grave. "Was that even a question?"

Gregson slid to a stop behind us and barked out, "Sanderson! Drop the wand, hands on your head. What tomfoolery is this?! Edwards, lower your weapon."

I turned my head just enough to explain the situation, as I didn't want him misjudging things. He didn't have the full context, after all. "Sanderson barged in here, attacking. He was in the middle of casting a Restricted Curse when Jamie burst in."

Gregson went from flabbergasted to outraged so quickly he likely gave himself emotional whiplash. "Edwards, I take it back, keep him in your sights. Sanderson, I won't repeat myself."

"Davenforth!" In a snap, Seaton appeared. Seaton had a wand up, looking about wildly, his hair and clothes mussed as if he'd portaled near here and then sprinted the rest of the distance. "What SOS? What happened—great dark magic, Sanderson! If you cast that spell, I will cut you down like a rabid dog. Drop it, now!"

I'd never been so relieved to see my friend. Bless him for not only portaling in, but doing so at the ready. He was indeed the man to call in an emergency.

"You're here. Of course he calls you here too." Sanderson puffed for breath, and his magic became unstable, jittery as he lost control over it. I tensed even further, ready to dive for the floor. Or behind Seaton—his shields might be up to the task. I'd drag

Gregson in with me. "He cost me everything, do you hear me! My license, my career, my reputation—it's all been dragged through the mud. You'd stand for him, knowing that?!"

"You really think he did any of that?" Seaton lifted his wand, and the spell he readied would not only decimate the man ready to curse us, but half the block as well. Sanderson, even as mad as he was in that moment, swallowed hard and fixated on the wand's tip. "Davenforth didn't destroy you, Sanderson. You didn't need his help to manage that. Now, I won't ask again. Dismiss the spell and give me your wand, or I cut you down where you stand."

Sanderson stared at us hard, his eyes darting from one face to the next, his rage a palpable thing. Still, some part of his survival instincts warned him doing anything more would be suicidal. He might have been able to best me alone, but he had no chance against all four of us. His wand slowly lowered and with it, the spell dissipated into thin air. The anger stayed flushed in his cheeks for a moment longer before draining slowly away, leaving him an unhealthy, waxy shade of grey. His eyes pinned on me like a belligerent child, not sure where he'd gone wrong, what misstep had landed him where he was. "She wouldn't stay, you know. If you lost your position, if your reputation was destroyed like mine was, she wouldn't stay with you."

Ah. Of course. The missing element to the picture. If he were dismissed, then he'd be a public embarrassment to his lady's father. Even if she could forgive him for it, her father wouldn't, and would have pressured her to break their understanding off. The betrayal and heartbreak of that could send any man over the edge. I unwillingly felt some sympathy for him.

He let the wand drop from his fingers. I drew a full breath as he did so, feeling like I could finally breathe once more. Sodding deities, but I never wanted to be that close to death again. Gregson scooted past and put him in cuffs himself, using the ones I had here to restrain a magic user. They were of the purest refined iron available and could stifle even a royal mage. The last of my dread dissipated, although it left me feeling hollow and shaky. Truly, near-death experiences left much to be desired.

Jamie uncocked her gun and let it hang by her side, regarding Sanderson in an unblinking, basilisk glare. "You fool. Your girlfriend breaking up with you isn't Henri's doing."

The man glared at us both venomously as Gregson marched him out of the room.

Seaton dismissed his spell as well, putting away the wand as he noted, "Good magic, man, it looks like a wrecking ball came through here."

"A wrecking ball with a name," I answered tartly. With Sanderson gone and in Gregson's care, I felt much more myself. I was more outraged than anything that the idiot had dared use me to unleash his anger upon.

Turning to me, Jamie's eyes swept over me from top to bottom. "You okay?"

"I'm well. A bit singed around the edges, perhaps, but well enough for all that."

She put an arm around me and hugged me tight, and I lingered for a moment. I needed a second to pull myself together, as the shock was just now hitting. I'd come far too close to staring death in the face just now. She smelt of sunshine and warm skin, and the tactile sensation soothed me as nothing else in the world could.

Seaton interrupted the moment by scooting around me, heading for the spectral energy spill. I mentally blessed him for being so quick-acting to clean that up. As he moved, he took a proper look behind my worktable, which was where the worst of the mess was. "Why in blazes would Sanderson come after you?

I know the two of you fight like sharks and dolphins, but this is a bit over the top, even for him."

"We'll need to report the whole thing to Gregson anyway. Just sit in and listen so he doesn't have to repeat himself," Jamie told her friend. She kept one hand on me, grip firm. I wasn't the only one rattled and needing a grounding touch, it seemed. "And after that, we head for the nearest decent bar."

"Great sodding deities, yes," I agreed on a long sigh. "I am in desperate need of a drink."

"First round's on me," Seaton promised.

Cleaning up this mess, not to mention the paperwork, would be tiresome in the extreme. But I was alive to deal with it, and I had two friends to thank for coming so immediately to my rescue. Really, I couldn't ask for anything more.

Report 19: At Least Things Can't Get Worse (Oh Wait)

It was near midnight by the time Gregson released Henri and I. Sherard still took us out to a bar afterwards—frankly, we all needed it—but we were so exhausted we barely got more than two rounds in before we opted for home. I steered Henri home by the elbows. He was completely done in and barely cognizant. He stumbled into his apartment on his own two feet, though, and gave me a sweet smile and goodnight before likely face-planting into his bed.

Mercy, what a day. I was rattled enough I didn't choose to immediately go to bed. I felt like nightmares and flashbacks loomed in my immediate future, and it wouldn't do me any good to close my eyes right now. It had been more than a little terrifying to see Sanderson pointing a wand at Henri, destruction all around them. Sanderson had looked insane, like a rabid dog. I honestly hadn't been sure if he'd stand down, even with me pointing a gun at him. It called up bad memories from my time on Earth, when I'd been in a similar situation. Only that time, I hadn't pulled out of it with everyone alive. Thank any god listening Henri had been safely extracted.

Feeling those dark memories resurfacing, I stayed up instead, recording in a journal everything that had happened. It was therapeutic, getting it all down on paper, even if the only person in this world who could read it was me.

By the time I got it all down, my mind settled, it was nearly two in the morning. I finally turned in, setting the alarm for nine, as Gregson had given us the morning off. We didn't need to be up until later, so I took advantage and slept as much as I could.

I didn't sleep well, flipping and flopping quite a bit, and

Clint gave up on staying anywhere near me an hour in. Still, I slept, which was better than I'd expected. Somewhere around eight, I woke up naturally and didn't feel like dozing. I was a bit worried for Henri. For all that he'd faced dangerous situations, it was a different thing to be ambushed in your own space, by a supposed colleague. I knew this from experience. When the mind was able to brace itself for danger, it handled the situation better. Being caught off guard rattled you down to your core.

With that idea in mind, I used the texting pad to contact him, as that seemed a nonintrusive way to check in. *Hey, you up?*

It took a good minute for him to respond, his handwriting less precise than normal. *Mostly.*

Want a breakfast burrito? Not that I had the ingredients for it. I'd have to run down to the corner market, but I was willing to do that.

If you're offering, I won't turn you down.

If he had, I'd have checked him into the nearest hospital. The day Henri turned down a homecooked meal, he was either on his deathbed, or he'd been kidnapped and was trying to signal me. *Thirty minutes, then come up.*

Will do.

I popped out, snagged the ingredients from the cheerful grocer—someone was having a good morning—and quickly retreated to my place. I stayed in jogging clothes, as I didn't feel like wearing a suit this morning. It was easier to cook in and far more comfortable. In short order I had several pans sizzling with meat and eggs, various veggies caramelizing in butter, and all the smells beyond tempting. Of course, my bloodhound partner followed the scents straight through my open door, a smile lighting his face as he came in.

One glance at him told the full story. For all his exhaustion, he hadn't slept well. There were dark circles under his eyes and a distinct drag to his feet. He was mostly dressed, his usual cravat and coat missing, hair still damp but combed. He hadn't been up long, then.

"Morning," I greeted, stirring eggs to keep them from scorching.

"Thank you for not saying 'good morning.'" He wearily dropped onto the bar stool across from me.

"Yeah, I'm not feeling a good morning. How are you, Henri?"

"I kept waking up and searching frantically for a wand," he answered with a grimace. "Panic dreams kept me up most of the night. I'm quite dead on my feet and not looking forward to writing that formal report of events. Gregson will need it to properly process Sanderson."

Oh yeah. I'd almost forgotten that. "I'll have Penny or Sherard help me write mine."

"Bless you. I won't have time to help you. Not if we're to get it done before we have to track down our suspect at the docks. And I still have to properly clean up and restore order to my lab." Henri wiped a hand over his face, looking quite ready to tumble back into bed. "Seaton did report something interesting to me this morning. He was alarmed enough at Sanderson's actions last night to do some digging."

I scraped eggs out of a skillet, ready to mix everything together to melt with the cheese, but gave him a go-ahead nod. "And?"

"Turns out there's a reason why Sanderson is so incompetent. He cheated in order to get his license."

My head came up sharply. "Dude! Seriously? Although I suppose it does explain a lot. Cheated how?"

"The final exam we all take in order to pass the qualifiers for a magical license? You know which one I mean?"

"Sure. It's the one you tested highest on, the test you beat Sherard's score in."

"That very one." He looked smug I'd remembered that. It was more like, Sherard still complained about it from time to time. "Sanderson paid someone else to take the test for him. There're protocols in place to prevent that sort of thing, but he'd found a way around them, apparently."

I let out a low whistle. "And let me guess. This all started coming to light when Sherard made that formal complaint, and people started to investigate Sanderson?"

"Basically." Henri lifted his shoulders in a lazy shrug. "As Seaton explained it to me, the investigator over the case questioned *why* someone so incompetent managed to maintain his position with the police. Hence why he investigated Sanderson's connection with the police commissioner. But the more he uncovered, the more he found to question, and eventually he went all the way back to Sanderson's magical license. So, in fact, Sanderson is in jeopardy of losing it all. I'd be very surprised if at the end of this week he'll have woman, job, or magical license to his name."

Shaking my head, I went back to pouring the yummy interior into a wrap, finishing our breakfasts. "You'd think if you'd cheated your way into a job with the police, you'd have enough sense to keep your head down."

"As we've already seen on multiple occasions, Sanderson is not capable of making good life decisions."

I snorted a laugh because it was so true. "At least he's out of your hair now. No one's going to make the argument that a cheating dastard with a volatile temper should be allowed to stay. Here." I set the plate in front of him with a soft clink. "I've got juice or sampni sun tea."

"Tea, please. I need it this morning."

Henri normally opted for tea. I was not a fan of this particular brand—it didn't really taste like sampni—but I kept a tin in the house for him. I fixed him a cup with two spoons of honey, the way he liked it. Henri accepted both plate and cup with a happy and inarticulate hum. A bear coming out of hibernation, presented with a feast of salmon and berries, could not have been happier. He was so easy to please.

I joined him on the other side of the bar, and for a time we just ate breakfast and let the world go by us. He popped up to make himself another one, then fixed one for me as well. It was definitely one of those days where we compensated the lack of sleep with food.

"So...what are you going to tell your parents about last

night?" I ventured as I accepted the plate from him.

Henri's expression looked pained from the very depths of his soul. "Must I?"

"You'd rather them hear it through rumor mill, when it gets totally blown out of proportion and your mother breaks into your apartment, convinced you're dying?" I countered.

"Deities preserve us, she would, too." He hunkered down into his seat, fixedly staring at nothing but his burrito. Finally, he muttered, "After breakfast."

"Okay," I agreed mildly. Hopefully he meant that. Otherwise, she really would break into his apartment.

We lost about three hours to writing reports and filing them to the right people. We had to submit triplicates to different agencies, as Sanderson was under professional investigation, and various people had to be notified. Henri finally did call his mother and gave her a very downplayed version of events. I listened in on this in amusement and he kept shooting me warning glares about interrupting him. Not that I would. Hearing him tap-dance around the truth like this was vastly entertaining. I mean, I'd witnessed part of that madness and I barely recognized the events he described.

By late afternoon, we'd managed to appease people long enough to go back to our investigation. It was a mite early for the *Windsprite* to be in, but better safe than sorry. I asked a few uniforms to help me canvass the docks, make sure we didn't lose him, but went down with Henri to talk to the man ourselves.

It was a rather nice summer's day, and being this close to the ocean, the breeze kept it cool. The docks were hoppin', ships coming in with the tide, cargo and passengers offloading, dockhands scurrying about. It made for interesting times trying to navigate it all without tripping over someone or getting knocked off into the water. I kept close to Henri as we made our way down. If I lost him in this crowd, I'd never find him again.

Halfway down, we found our ship. It was another six-mast trading ship with a massive hull. I understood this to not be unusual—windwhisperers were almost exclusively used for ships of this size to keep them moving on the open ocean. Still, I had to wonder what that did to poor Martin, to once again be on a ship of the same class and size not a month after almost dying on one. Surely the man had PTSD from the experience. Was it wise to put him on a ship again this soon?

We found a corner of the dock, near the gangplank, to stop and wait. I had a brief description of what Martin looked like, but really, we were watching for his uniform. He'd be wearing the light blue and white tunic and loose pants of a sailor, and the three blue stripes on his sleeve to mark him as a windwhisperer.

"Which do you think it will be?" Henri mused to me in a low tone, barely audible above the din of the crowd around us. "Will he flee like a guilty man or talk with us?"

"I honestly have no idea. I'm still not sure he did it. All we've got is circumstantial evidence at this point."

"True. Just because he's the only one who looks guilty doesn't mean it's him." Henri gave me a sidelong look. "But you do think it's him."

"Gut instinct. And we haven't found anyone else with the right motive, timing, and magical ability. If it's not him, we're going to be up a creek with no paddle."

Henri's mouth curved into an approving smile. "Look at you, using aquatic metaphors."

I rolled my eyes at him in exasperation. "Henri, I hate to break this to you, but that one's from Earth."

"Is it really?"

"We *do* have seven oceans, you know. Your people didn't invent bodies of water—oh hey, is that him?"

Henri perked up and looked where I did, spying the compact blond with a sailor's long duffle bag slung over his shoulder. "He's got the stripes and right look, at least. Let's call out to him."

Since I'm naturally louder than my quiet partner, I did the honors. "Mr. Robert Martin!"

Sure enough, his head turned and he looked at us askance. Something about us must have said 'cop' to him. His eyes widened and he turned and immediately bolted.

I swore, even as I started chasing him, Henri on my heels. Well, at least, he tried. No one on this planet who was purely human could keep up with me at full speed. Martin only kept his head start because he kept plowing through groups of people, upsetting them, and blocking my path of pursuit. I grimly kept at it, leaping over displaced crates, downed people, and anything else that got in my way.

He tossed several wind spells over his shoulder, trying to knock me over or slow me down. Because there was magic in the wind, I was immune to the attack, and I kept running without issue. That spooked him properly and he ran even harder after that.

The cool breeze didn't keep me from warming up, and I was overheating quickly in the jacket, but I didn't pause to take it off. I was gaining on him slowly, and with every look back, Martin cost himself an extra two seconds. I grinned wolfishly. It was human instinct to keep track of your pursuers, but it really did cost people in the long run.

Maybe he sensed he'd be down in a few seconds. I didn't know for sure, but he suddenly planted his feet and turned, the expression on his face ugly. It was the look of a man cornered, one so desperate he didn't care about the consequences. I'd seen that expression on people's faces before, and nothing good had followed.

I had my gun half out of its holster on sheer instinct, knowing he was about to do something dangerous and stupid. "Martin, drop to the ground! Hands above your head!"

He didn't. He reached into his pocket, and I didn't need the glint of sunlight on metal to know he'd just taken out a bullet.

Henri was several paces behind, puffing like the little engine that could, struggling to catch up. Still, he saw it too, or surmised it somehow. He let out a howl and I could feel his magic slam around me, glimmering like stardust. A shield of some kind.

It made no difference. The bullet shot from Martin's hand, flying straight to me, sneaking under Henri's shield by milimeters. I instinctively tried to roll away from it, but even my reflexes weren't faster than a bullet. It hit me dead in the hip, the impact of it spinning me around. I landed hard on the cobblestone, dizzy with it, heartbeat pounding like a war drum.

I instinctively clapped a hand over the area shot, expecting the wet and sticky feeling of blood. There was no pain, but injuries sometimes took a second—the instinctual panic receded and I abruptly remembered I was bulletproof now. It was the one upside to Belladonna's magical alterations on me: I was essentially Superwoman.

I didn't cackle as I got an elbow under me, but it was a near thing. I did poke at my hip experimentally, and while the impact of it smarted like crazy, the bullet hadn't penetrated the skin.

But just because I was bulletproof, it didn't mean anything else was. I stared down in dismay at the hole in my pants and the shirt tucked under it. "These are my favorite pants!" I wailed in protest.

Martin stared at me in stunned surprise. No doubt because I wasn't flailing on the docks or bleeding or screaming or any of the other things that people would normally do when shot at. That moment of stillness cost him.

Henri shot off a spell and ropes appeared from nowhere, wrapping around the man and taking him down like a flying tackle. Martin hit the stone docks hard, his chin clipping audibly, and no doubt rattling his brain and teeth. I got over my pants and went to him, slapping an iron set of cuffs on his wrists to shut his magic off. Just in case.

"You idiot," I told the downed suspect with disgust.

"Shooting a police officer does not help your case, not one iota. And now you've pissed off both me *and* Henri and let me tell you, we weren't having a good morning to begin with."

Turning his head, he glared at me and spat out blood. Bit his tongue, had he? Or his cheek. Something. "You think I care? After what I did?"

Well, well, someone was unhinged. "You can tell me all about it at the station. Up we come."

He struggled unhelpfully, much like a worm on a hook, as I hauled him upright. Henri caught up to me and gave me a once over, saw the bullet wound and his glare turned lethal.

"You're fine?" he demanded of me.

"Of course I'm not fine, do you know how much these pants cost? And how hard it is to find pants that are wide enough in the hips and yet long enough for my legs? It's like finding a unicorn!"

"So, in other words, the bullet just bounced off you." He grumbled inarticulately, but I could hear the relief clear enough. Then he turned that glare on Martin. "With what possible logic would it seem a good idea to fire at a police detective? Are you trying to ensure you're locked away for the next hundred years?"

Even if that hadn't been his goal, he'd managed it. Just killing a royal mage had done that. And after this whole running stunt and firing a bullet with a wind spell, I had no doubt this was our man.

Martin glared back and stubbornly kept his mouth shut.

Shaking my head, I hauled him bodily towards the main road, where I'd left the car parked. "Come on, you. We've got a lot of questions that need answers."

Magic Outside the Box

Jamie, we need to sort out your priorities. Paws, really?

excuse you very much, my priorities are just fine

When you're shot in front of your partner, you should first
reassure them you're not hurt.

fine fine

"Fine, fine," she says.

you're so salty—want some fries with that salt?

Report 20: Confession

Normally when Jamie and I sat in the same interrogation room, we traded off and played good-cop, bad-cop. Since I was generally more genial, I often took on the role of good-cop. Unfortunately, neither of us were in the mood to be 'good' in any sense of the word, and today Martin got bad-cop, worse-cop.

I'd try to feel regretful about that later.

Martin didn't seem at all inclined to put up a defense. He sat at the table with his arms crossed belligerently, glaring darkly at anyone who dared to meet his eyes. Seaton and McSparrin both crowded up against the side of the room, silent spectators, and he seemed to pay them little to no attention. For whatever reason, he kept his attention mostly on Jamie. It might have been because a bullet had just bounced off of her.

It was a startling sight, even for someone who understood the reasons behind it. I'd known, intellectually, a bullet couldn't harm her. Yet my heart had still threatened to choke me when I saw that bullet wing from his hand. Would there ever come a time when I saw danger approach her, danger I knew she was immune to, and not be terrified? I somehow doubted it.

Needless to say, Jamie glared at Martin, Martin stared right back at her, and I glared at him. It was a fine tableau this evening.

Jamie didn't slam her hands against the table, or try to startle him in any way. She just leaned one elbow against the surface and locked eyes with him. "You killed Joseph Burtchell."

Martin's generous mouth lifted up in a sneer. "I ain't apologizin' for it, if that's what you're fishin' for. Man had it comin'."

My hands spasmed in my lap. Deities, but I wanted to fling a curse at him for the callousness alone.

A tic developed in my partner's jaw. "Why did you kill him?"

"Ain't that obvious enough? Man let me whole crew drown." The horror from that night washed over his expression and his eyes went blind for a moment, his head locked in the past. "He saves them fancy, important people first, because what else do you expect from the likes of him? Retired royal mage and all. And he lets us poor sailors drown like we ain't nothin' but rats. And he gets *praised* for it, for saving three ships and not the other two. Every time I heard those praises, I lost my mind."

His hands came up, as if he wanted to grip his head, but the manacles around his wrists prevented the movement. He dropped his hands again, staring at them as if he didn't recognize his own limbs. His voice almost turned singsong, remembered agony roughening his tone. "No one understood what it was like, drownin'. The cold sea goin' over your head, and the waters being so dark you couldn' tell up from down. Of not knowin' if you could get breath, and your lungs seizin' for the lack of air. I was desperate for air. *Me*, a windwhisperer, of all people. I couldn' even get wind to help me out, because water had its death grip on me. Sheer luck I managed to latch onto what was left of the mast, heave meself out of the water."

Was this a form of depression, after surviving such a horrific accident? I'd seen cases where the survivors were so eaten up by guilt they eventually took their own lives. I'd seen people who lived through a traumatic experience and needed someone—anyone—to blame. To hate. It was the only way for them to make sense of what they'd lived through.

Martin seemed to fall in the latter category. I stared at him, dumbfounded by the depths at which the human mind could fall, how twisted a man could become from tragedy. If he'd been an impartial bystander to that same event, he likely would have said what everyone else in Sheffield had—how lucky they'd been that Burtchell was on hand. How it was less of a tragedy, as the man had at least saved three. It was the difference between the survivor and the spectator. And the defining line of murder.

It was incredibly sad, really. If someone had noticed and helped Martin work through his rage, would it have come to this? I shook my head, anger and resignation churning in my gut. The what-if's didn't matter. The deed was done, the bridge burned, and there was no way to bring a dead man back.

I wasn't interested in explaining to him how wrong he'd been to murder Burtchell. Any logic or pleas to reason would have fallen on deaf ears. Martin was in no way receptive to hearing he was wrong. And frankly, it didn't matter. This man would never see the outside of a prison again. Queen Regina would make sure of it. If she didn't have him executed. I personally bet on the latter. Queen Regina was not in a forgiving state of mind.

Jamie abruptly stood and left the room entirely. I saw no further reason to sit and listen to Martin either. We knew how he'd done it. We'd suspected why. Having the confirmation of 'who' was all we needed in this case. I pushed my chair back and stood, signaling for the other two to go ahead of me.

"Wait, that's it?" Martin's chair rattled as he jerked around, tone rising incredulously. "That's all you're going to ask?"

"You killed a man in cold blood," Seaton informed him with icy disdain. "We only needed your confession."

Martin, for some reason, reacted as if we should have been hanging off his every word. As if we needed him to walk us through it all. His jaw flapped for a moment before he spluttered, "But you don't know how I got in and out! Or how I killed him!"

"You really think we didn't figure any of it out?" McSparrin demanded, one hand on her hip, a classic picture of pity and exasperation. "We knew who to look for, didn't we? Oh, aye, you were clever enough to sneak through the gaps in his guard. But you're not a genius and these two gentlemen *are*. You were doomed the minute you decided to kill a nice, retired mage for daring to help people in their hour of need. I personally hope the queen doesn't hang you for it and instead lets you rot in prison for a very long time."

Her piece said, McSparrin stomped out of the room. I couldn't top a grander exit, so I followed her out, locking the door behind me. I'd have to guard him until we could put him in a proper magical jail. He had enough magic to cause trouble for a non-magical jailer.

Seaton put his shoulders to the wall opposite the door, settling in. I mirrored him because frankly, carrying about my own body weight was too exhausting after the events of yesterday and this afternoon. The brick felt cool against my shoulders and I felt a yawn stretch my face. Great magic, but I'd be happy to tumble into my bed tonight.

"My grandmother once said revenge was akin to drinking poison to quench your thirst. I don't think I truly understood that until just now." Seaton passed a weary hand over his face.

"That was your first thought, eh? Mine was something else. Earth has an expression Jamie uses often: No good deed goes unpunished."

Snorting, Seaton splayed a hand in silent agreement.

Silence fell for a moment before he asked, "Where is Jamie, anyway?"

"I assumed she was updating the queen that we'd caught our murderer." She was taking a tad longer to do that than she should have. Then again, Gregson would need to know as well. She could have been waylaid.

Seaton snorted in black amusement and leaned in to murmur, "Did you know, Weiss was still going through archived cases, looking for a suspect this morning? He was irate I wouldn't call you three in to help him. I told him you had that kerfuffle from yesterday to deal with and that I thought he was barking up the wrong tree besides. He didn't take it well. Imagine what the look on his face will be when he hears we caught the man?"

A very uncharitable smile lit my face. "It's a pity we won't see it in person. Oh great magic, I just realized. Since we solved this case, the queen's going to be even more firm in her stance in making us consultants to the kingsmen."

Seaton practically purred, "Why yes, she is."

I gave him a sidelong glance. Seaton, after all, was over the kingsmen. Weiss might be their commander, but Seaton was their minister, which put them on more or less equal stations. A suspicion I'd harbored for some time seemed more likely with every passing moment. "Seaton. Be honest with me. Was it your idea or the queen's to have Jamie be a consultant?"

"Mutual," he corrected me with a winsome smile. "It was a mutual idea. Great minds think alike and all that."

Hogwash.

Speaking of, my partner strolled down the hallway toward us with that smooth stride and a smug grin on her face. "Queen Regina wants to talk to our prisoner tomorrow. Well, she said talk; I'm more inclined to think she's going to verbally slice him to ribbons.

Anyway, we need to stash him properly tonight. Weiss is up in arms that we made an arrest without him. I told him where he could take his opinion and stuff it."

In her mood, she likely hadn't been polite about it, either. "And Captain Gregson?"

"Updated him while I was updating the queen. He's both pleased and relieved. Says we can go home after we get our guy processed."

No wonder she'd been a bit delayed getting back to us. "Then let's be about it."

We were invited for breakfast the next morning with Queen Regina. Well, I say 'invited' but there really was no choice in the matter. Kingsman Gibson came and fetched us himself, and a smirk played around his mouth as he watched my fidgeting in the carriage. Jamie—who was resplendent in a white dress that quite flattered her golden skin and figure—didn't seem at all alarmed at this abrupt summons. Then again, she knew Queen Regina far better than I.

Jamie's hand caught mine before I could tug at the sleeves of my coat again. "Stop. We're not in trouble."

I shot her a glower. "I didn't think we were."

"You're not in trouble," Gibson seconded, and his smirk widened a bit. "Quite the opposite. Our revered queen wants to offer you a job. She seems to think if she does it in person, you have less chance of finding a way to duck out of it."

A job? Oh, he must mean the consultant position. Having an answer to my worries calmed my nerves and I didn't feel the need to vibrate out of my skin. "Is that what this is about?"

"What did you think it was about?" Gibson inquired,

mildly curious. The burly kingsman looked entirely presentable in his red coat, and his hair perfectly combed. I found that irritating, along with his casual slouch in the seat, as if he hadn't a care in the world. Because of course he didn't.

"Gibson." I favored him with a pointed look and an arch of my eyebrow. "I've seen our queen face to face exactly twice. The first time, it was after that charms fiasco, which was well on its way to devastating the city population. The second time, she told me a retired royal mage had been mysteriously murdered. And you're wondering why I'm nervous about being abruptly summoned to see her again?"

"Ah. Well, in that context…" He shrugged, affably and with something that might have been a soft chuckle. "But no disaster looms ahead of you today."

Thank all deities for that.

The palace stretched out ahead of us. We were in the prime slot of the morning for heavy rush hour traffic, and it took much longer than it should have to cross the last distance and into the palace grounds themselves. I immediately saw why Gibson had come to fetch us, as he was the one who had the authority to admit us onto palace grounds. He was also the person who understood where the queen's favorite morning parlor was, and where she normally took her breakfast.

I walked through the many, many hallways of the palace, past all the white walls with their gold-painted trim and elaborate moldings, the priceless art upon the walls, the statues and water fountains resting in alcoves, and knew I'd be hopelessly lost if not for our escort. It was all lovely and majestic, to be sure, but it also became rather repetitive after a certain point. I didn't think myself directionally challenged until faced with a four-story building taking up three city blocks.

Gibson led us toward the back of the building (I think; at least, the morning light coming in through the windows suggested such) and to a nondescript wooden door that stood halfway open. He gave a perfunctory knock against the wood. It was abruptly opened the rest of the way by a woman in the sharp red and black uniform of the palace guard. She gave him a nod and then stepped back, allowing us all the room necessary to walk through.

"Oh, here already? Excellent, I was afraid it would take longer." Queen Regina stood from her seat at the small, round table and welcomed us with a brilliant smile. "Dr. Davenforth, Detective, do come in."

I doffed my hat and gave her a bow of greeting. Jamie smoothly curtseyed before rising. "Your Majesty."

"Come sit," she invited again, her hand gesturing to the three settings already placed and waiting. "I do apologize for the abruptness of my invitation, but I needed to hear all the details myself."

"Quite alright, I wasn't able to tell you everything over the pad last night," Jamie responded. She approached the table as if she were dining with any other friend. The queen looked pleased by her attitude.

Not able to let my partner outdo me, I copied her behavior and sat where the queen pointed. Servants appeared from the woodwork to serve us all an excellent omelet, a side of small fruit crepes, and dark-roasted coffee. The coffee especially was welcome, and I drank of it deeply. I needed all my brain cells firing for this conversation.

After we were served, Queen Regina started firing off questions. Jamie and I took turns answering them, so we could eat and speak without being rude about it. Only when she was satisfied she had all the particulars did the queen's full attention turn toward me.

"I'm surprised, Dr. Davenforth, that you know every nook and cranny as well as Detective Edwards does. Do you investigate alongside her throughout a case?"

She was not the first to wonder or question this. I patiently answered, "For the most part, yes. We will occasionally split up, if our talents are better served following a lead in different directions, or if we have others working the case with us, we'll mix up partners. It depends on the circumstances. On this last case, for instance, Seaton and I took the issue of the wards and the bullet on while the women interviewed all the witnesses. We played to our individual strengths."

"How interesting. But you're not trained to be a flatfoot."

"No, I am not. I've learned to follow my partner's lead and acquired a great deal about the investigative process in the interim."

"I see." This answer set the wheels of thought in motion. I could almost hear the gears turning in her mind.

"It's actually quite helpful for me too," Jamie put in casually, sipping at the remains of her coffee. She sat quite at her leisure in the chair, looking entirely elegant and self-assured. "I know so little about magic and what all it can do, I often don't think to question if it's there. The glasses they issue at the department can see it, but it doesn't really tell me much except where a magical presence is. Henri, of course, can not only see it but dissect it."

"Yes, I can imagine how that would be beneficial during an investigation. My own kingsmen are normally magicians for that reason. That, and the dangers they face often require magical expertise to defend against." Queen Regina put her fork down with a deliberateness that did not escape me. It seemed we were now on the second part of her agenda. "Aside from hearing the details of Joseph's case, I wanted to speak with you more candidly on another matter. Jamie, I've asked you this before. I'll ask it again. Will you join my kingsmen?"

Jamie pursed her lips and didn't answer immediately. My heart beat loudly enough I felt sure everyone in the room could hear it.

Queen Regina's expression went mildly wicked, as she turned up the flames a bit higher. "Of course I mean that invitation for both you and Dr. Davenforth. Doctor, you've proven to be both adaptable and competent. I adore that combination beyond reasoning. It's why I've continually invited Jamie to join us. I understood her hesitancy to do so, and I've not pushed, but I do wish for her knowledge and expertise to be more readily available to me."

And Jamie had made it clear already that she didn't want to join without me. I cast Jamie a glance, not sure if she'd changed her mind since we last spoke of this. I found the idea intriguing, to be frank. The work would surely be interesting and I did adore a good mental challenge. My position at the precinct was becoming routine and predictable. I wouldn't mind a change of pace.

Something of this must have shown on my face as Jamie perked up, her eyebrows lifting into her hairline. "Really?"

A wide smile crossed my face. "I'm game if you are."

"Well, if you put it like *that...*" she demurred and then saucily winked at me.

Queen Regina clapped her hands together, looking back and forth between us with a hopeful expression. "Yes? Is that a yes?"

"Provisionally," Jamie answered, waving her down. "I still think I'm a bit too new to this world to leap into the fray. Let's start as consultants, see how well that works. In another year, we can come back to this question and revisit it."

She was so pleased to finally get an agreement, Queen Regina immediately nodded without any hesitation. "Done. I'll put forth the correct orders and paperwork for you immediately. Both Gibson and Sherard have told me point blank that if you agreed, you'd work directly with them. Is that acceptable?"

More than. It eased my nerves as well, as I knew I could work well with both of them. "I'd be delighted to work with them."

"Same," Jamie agreed forthrightly. "I assume we'll need a little training about kingsmen protocol before we start?"

Gibson, still standing at the ready near the door, cleared his throat. "I'll handle that."

More protocols to memorize. I mentally sighed in resignation. "And what of Weiss?"

Queen Regina's jaw jutted out in a stubborn tilt. "He answers to me. They are, after all, MY kingsmen."

And I was not fool enough to follow that up with another question.

Her good humor returned and she clapped her hands together again. The queen was too dignified to bounce in her chair, but I had the notion she was on some internal level. "I'm so happy you both agreed! I look forward to working with you."

I looked to my partner, noted the bright smile on her face, and shared it with one of my own. "So are we."

Jamie's Additional Report: Aftermath

Two months later

Ellie and I giggled like teenage girls over a boy as we offloaded the new motorcycle. She'd put together a sidecar according to my descriptions, so the motorcycle wasn't quite the two-wheeler I'd initially requested. But Ellie deserved to be along for the test ride, and really, if the thing broke down partway through this test, we'd need her and her tools to fix it again.

She popped into the sidecar while I threw a leg over the bike, getting settled. I wore a helmet and goggles because I wasn't an idiot, and because this country road had more curves than a hag's wrinkled face. Starting the engine, I listened to it purr, a wicked smile crossing over my face.

Of course Ellie caught it and she giggled again, settling her tool bag between her feet. "You're going to punch it, aren't you?"

"Duh. Of course." I looked at the speedometer as I revved the beauty up. This lovely machine could do eighty, an unheard-of thing in this world, and I literally could not wait to go a proper speed for once. "Ready?"

Ellie threw a fist into the air. "Go!"

I put both legs up against the bike and hit the throttle wide open, pouring on the gas. We didn't pop a wheelie, not with the sidecar attached, but I could hear the tires spin before they caught traction against the pavement. The bike took off in a shot and I laughed when we passed fifty. The wind in my face felt good, the speed of the bike even better, and I barely slowed for the curves at all.

My friend gripped the front of the car, but not in a death grip, not like certain people would have done. There was a wide smile on her face too, and she seemed entranced by the speed.

I drove and let the sensations of countryside, mowed grass, summer heat and the vibrations of the motor between my legs wash over me. For a moment, just a moment, I felt like I'd never left home. That I was on Earth, with a good friend next to me, and nothing but the open road ahead of us. Then a motorcar crested the hill, spoiling the illusion. A pang hit my heart but it was alright. I was more or less re-signed to being in this world now. And I couldn't unwish being here.

Shaking off the strange mood, I saw a gravelly pull-off area to the right, near a four-road crossing. I slowed and pulled over, letting the engine idle. "How is it?"

"She's running like a dream," Ellie responded, practically bouncing in her seat. "I want a go."

"Well yeah, she's your baby too." I swung off and we switched places so Ellie could drive for a while. As I settled, my knees tucked up against my chest, I asked her, "Anything you want to change?"

"I think the tires need to be a little wider, like you sug-gested. Not sure where we'd get them made, but I'll track a supplier down." She patted the bike with a proud stroke of fingers over the gauges. "And I think the brakes could use some adjustment. You're having to brake far ahead of where you need to stop."

'Modern' brakes weren't used to stopping anything go-ing at this speed, so it made sense. "I think the steering needs a bit of tightening, too."

"Oh? Alright, let me feel it for myself." Ellie cast me a glance as she casually promised, "I think I can get you your own bike done in another month or so. Need a sidecar to go with it?"

Something about the way she asked got my curiosity up. "Well, yeah. I might need it at some point."

A smirk toyed around Ellie's mouth. "For Henri."

I snorted at the idea. "Henri? You think I'll be able to get Henri in this thing? He'll see it as a deathtrap and find reasons to avoid it."

"You really think so?" Her smirk widened to the point of being enigmatic. "I think he'll climb in if you're the one asking."

Just what was she hinting at...? No, never mind. I'd figure it out later. "I guess we'll see, won't we? You ready?"

"Absolutely." Ellie revved the engine and cackled. We took off once more, the bike steadily gaining speed as Ellie adjusted to going over thirty miles an hour. When she hit eighty, the engine roaring, I saw her light up under the goggles and knew an adrenaline addict had just been born. Or maybe reborn was the proper way to say it.

Either way, suggesting a bike that could go over a hundred would be an easy sell.

Settling back, I laughed and enjoyed the ride.

hundred

A HUNDRED?! Crap. I thought you were done with this one.
Why are you re-reading it?

Stay on topic, you madwoman.

Why in the wide green world would you need to go a
HUNDRED MILES AN HOUR?

Because I can? Actually, Henri, while I have you, answer the question:
Would you ride in the sidecar?

I, well, only if you insist.

SERIOUSLY?! I thought I was the crazy one in this relationship.

Perhaps this isn't the time to question my mental shortcomings.
The fact I would obviously follow you anywhere does not
bode well for our chances of survival.

Awww. I love you too. You're blushing reading this, aren't you?

Oh do stop.

Jamie's Notes to Herself:

• Sampni — it's a fruit, kinda a mix between mango and passionfruit. Really yummy. I can drink my weight in this tea, no kidding.

• Cold tea — is not a thing here. Kingston views cold tea the way the Brits back home think of cold tea. America, WHAT ARE YOU DOING kind of outrage. I think I might have to give this one up as a lost cause.

• FINALLY FOUND SOY SAUCE. It comes from a tree, oddly enough. Kinda like a maple extract.

Air quality in Kingston is starting to get bad. I remember reading that the air quality around the major cities during the Industrial Revolution was really awful. I now see what they mean. I've got a bug in Ellie's ear about putting an air purifier on the mufflers of the cars. Maybe I can put another bug in Queen Regina's ear too?

I have found the equivalent of IKEA. Only it's a magical store. It is APPALLING how that place is laid out. I was lost in there for hours until Sherard rescued me. I learned very quickly that you cannot trust the arrows painted on the floor; that if you mispronounce any of the product names, you can accidentally summon demons; and worse, walls shift and appear out of nowhere! I refuse to go back in there again.

Kingstonisms:

• At a rate of knots – to go at top speed, or driving very fast

• Dead on end – when something is lined up perfectly with something else

• Don't hand me a line – when someone is too busy talking and not actually doing the work

• Dragging your anchor – being impeded by something or acting in a tired manner

• Flogging the glass – leaving your watch ahead of schedule, originated by shaking an hour glass to make time go by faster

• A fluky – light wind that doesn't blow steadily from any direction, variable

• In the drink – someone who has fallen into the water

• Leading light – someone who marks the way or is a leader, comes from it being customary to mark the entry to a port with a line of leading lights to show the way

• Coddiwomple – to travel purposefully to an as of yet unknown destination

Days of the Week

Earth – Draiocht

Sunday – Gods Day

Monday – Gather Day

Tuesday – Brew Day

Wednesday – Bind Day

Thursday – Hex Day

Friday – Scribe Day

Saturday – Rest Day

Months

Earth – Draiocht

January – Old Moon

February – Snow Moon

March – Crow Moon

April – Seed Moon

May – Hare Moon

June – Rose Moon

July – Hay Moon

August – Corn Moon

September – Harvest Moon

October – Hunter's Moon

November – Frost Moon

December – Blue Moon

Werespecies: werehorses,   wereowls,   weremules, werefoxes, weredogs, werebadgers, wererabbits, werewolves

Thanks for reading *Magic Outside the Box*! Ready for the next adventure?

Breaking and Entering 101

Other books by Honor Raconteur
Published by Raconteur House
♫ Available in Audiobook! ♫

THE ADVENT MAGE CYCLE
Jaunten ♫
Magus ♫
Advent ♫
Balancer ♫

ADVENT MAGE NOVELS
Advent Mage Compendium
The Dragon's Mage ♫
The Lost Mage

WARLORDS (ADVENT MAGE)
Warlords Rising
Warlords Ascending
Warlords Reigning

ANCIENT MAGICKS
Rise of the Catalyst♫

THE ARTIFACTOR SERIES
The Child Prince ♫
The Dreamer's Curse ♫
The Scofflaw Magician ♫
The Canard Case ♫
The Fae Artifactor ♫

THE CASE FILES OF HENRI DAVENFORTH
Magic and the Shinigami Detective ♫
Charms and Death and Explosions (oh my) ♫
Magic Outside the Box ♫
Breaking and Entering 101 ♫
Three Charms for Murder
Grimoires and Where to Find Them
Death Over the Garden Wall
This Potion is Da Bomb
All in a Name
A Matter of Secrets and Spies

DEEPWOODS SAGA
Deepwoods ♫
Blackstone
Fallen Ward
Origins
Crossroads
Jioni

FAMILIAR AND THE MAGE
The Human Familiar
The Void Mage
Remnants
Echoes

GÆLDORCRÆFT FORCES
Call to Quarters

IMAGINEERS
Imagineer
Excantation

KINGMAKERS
Arrows of Change ♫
Arrows of Promise
Arrows of Revolution

KINGSLAYER
Kingslayer ♫
Sovran at War ♫

SINGLE TITLES
Special Forces 01
Midnight Quest

THE TOMES OF KALERIA
Tomes Apprentice ♫
First of Tomes ♫
Master of Tomes ♫

File X: Author

Honor Raconteur was born loving books. Her mother read her fairy tales and her father read her technical manuals, so was it any wonder she grew up thinking all books were wonderful? At five, she wrote and illustrated her first book.

At *mumbles age* she's lost count of how many books she's written and has no intention of stopping before she climbs into a grave. Right now, she lives in Michigan in a wonderful old Craftsman house with two dogs, three cats, and a fish.

For more information about her books, to be notified when books are released, or get behind the scenes info about upcoming books, sign up for her newsletter at honorraconteur.news@raconteurhouse.com

www.honorraconteur.com
FB: Honor Raconteur's Book Portal
Patreon

Made in United States
Troutdale, OR
01/15/2024

16955353R00126